ONE WHOPPER OF A LOVE STORY

A SWEET ROMANTIC COMEDY

NEVER SAY NEVER
BOOK SEVEN

REMI CARRINGTON

❀ Created with Vellum

They say you have to kiss a lot of frogs, but what if a prince shows up . . .

When a prince—not the kind who wears a crown—swoops in to rescue me, I kiss him before I even ask his name. I'm sure I've given him the wrong impression, and he'll bolt away like a cat out of a bathtub.

Except he keeps showing up.

Maybe fairy tales are real.

We all know that isn't true.

CHAPTER 1

LAYLA

$\mathcal{I}$ was supposed to turn left when I saw the donkeys. But there weren't any donkeys near that corner even though it felt like my turn. Maybe they'd wandered back to the barn. That idea didn't occur to me until just now. Dang it.

Choosing a landmark that couldn't move would have been smarter.

Leaning forward, I scanned the landscape. Nothing looked familiar, but I'd been looking at the donkeys, not the barn. I probably should have trusted my gut and turned left back there.

"Are you still there, Layla?" Lettie asked.

I adjusted the phone in the holder. The flimsy plastic holder wasn't doing a great job of keeping my phone still. There was probably a loose screw or something. "Yeah. Just a bit lost." I sipped my Vanilla Dr Pepper. If anything could get the gray matter firing, it was Dr Pepper. "But anyway, it wasn't a kids party."

"What? Someone booked a mermaid for an adult par—oh!" Lettie gasped. "What happened?"

"Nothing really. A few guys got a little handsy. But one guy—I almost gave him my number but then remembered that I'd given up impulsivity this year—told me where the back door was, then distracted the guys so I could slip out. I'm just mad. And lost. How many stupid little roads are there in the Hill Country?"

"Do you want a count of all roads or just the stupid ones?"

"Not helpful. What was really funny was stopping at Sonic. I got one of the really big drinks, and you'd think a mermaid had never pulled through the drive-thru before." I didn't bother to tell her that not even a mile down the road, I'd managed to drop the lid onto the floorboard and was now living dangerously with a large open cup in my car. It was begging to be spilled.

She laughed. "You're probably the first. But the guy who helped sounds nice. Maybe you should have given him your number."

"First of all, it's only February, and my resolution was to curb impulsiveness for a whole year. Second, if he's hanging out with all those guys, I'm not sure I want him to have my number."

"True. Well, I'm sorry it was a flop. You going to be okay?"

"Absolutely. I'm going to pull a U-turn when I find a wide spot, then head home and get out of this costume." Or maybe I could find my way to Stadtburg by a different road. I spotted a small road on the left and turned, hoping something would start to look familiar. If not, I'd turn around.

At least it wasn't dark. Yet.

If it weren't for that stupid frat party, I wouldn't be lost in the maze of paved cow paths. What sort of overgrown boys booked a mermaid for their friend's birthday party? Two minutes after I'd arrived, it had been evident that my definition of entertainment and their definition differed greatly. If they'd wanted a stripper, they should have hired one. My talents included making balloon animals—just dogs and flowers—and singing children's songs. I'd tried making the other balloon animals, but they took more skill than I could muster. All I had for my hours of practice were lots of popped balloons and a wicked startle reflex.

I pulled to the edge of the road and opened my phone. It was time to get help from my map app. After studying the screen and turning my phone in a complete circle until I was pretty sure that left meant south, I stuck the phone back in the holder. The plastic gadget was cheap, but it mostly did the job of holding my phone.

With the radio turned down, I eased back onto the road and kept going, inching along and hoping for a familiar landmark.

A board appeared in the road out of nowhere, and I didn't react fast enough to actually avoid it. The bump knocked my phone loose from the holder, and my pretty little phone landed in my over-sized cup with a horrifying splash.

I grabbed the top of the cup, slammed on the brakes, and somehow managed not to spill Dr Pepper everywhere. With my foot on the brake, I fished my phone out and dropped the dripping wet phone into the cupholder.

When I passed a store, I'd buy rice. I could only hope that would save my phone. Getting a new one right now wasn't in my budget.

I eased back onto the road, but something wasn't right. The car leaned funny, and there was a thumping sound when I moved. I sped up, and the thump became more frequent. I slowed down, and the noise slowed. After less than two minutes, I pulled off to the side again. This time I made sure I was all the way into the grass.

Holding my tail up out of the grass, I waddled around to the passenger side. A flat tire.

There wasn't much I could do about it dressed like this. Even in normal clothes, I wasn't good at changing a tire. I knew the basics of how, but the last time I'd tried, I hadn't been able to undo the lug nuts or whatever those things are called.

This was a bad time to have a wet phone. How long would it take for it to dry out enough to use? Too long.

My grand plan for starting over in Stadtburg, where almost no one knew me, wasn't going horribly, but great wasn't the word I'd use to describe it either.

My tendency toward giggling and impulsive decisions was often misinterpreted, and I hated being labeled as stupid. If I were tall and had no curves, would the same assumptions be made?

With a wet phone and a flat tire, I had few options. My best option was to walk to get help. Probably my only option. But I didn't like that option since I was wearing a mermaid costume.

As I waddled down the road with my lobster purse hooked over my shoulder, I assessed my recent choices. They weren't all stupid.

For instance, the lobster purse was perfect with this outfit. It added to the theme. Besides, who didn't love lobster? I liked mine with butter and served beside a steak.

Going to breakfast with the older hottie I'd met in the grocery store was a mistake. Dating someone in their fifties was a bad idea in general. But I'd ignored his age because he was tall and broad shouldered, and I had a thing for tall and broad-shouldered men. He'd also had steaks in his shopping cart, but no lobster.

Because I was short, tall included a lot of men.

At least the old guy had been a gentleman, and he was a fabulous cook. Best steak I'd ever had. That shouldn't have been surprising since he was a chef, but because he looked like a rancher, I'd been shocked. His friends were nice though. I saw them from time to time around town. I saw him too, but he'd only nod, then find someplace else to focus.

It was obvious he thought inviting me over had been a mistake.

Thinking about my bad decisions would only depress me. And considering I was waddling along the side of the road in a mermaid costume, I didn't need that right now. This was an all-around bad day.

Good decisions. I needed to think about my good decisions. Brightening the lives of children was a great thing, but that hadn't ended well. I needed to think about a good decision that didn't include a downside.

Working at the doughnut shop.

Applying to work at Sweet's was a great decision. I'd been there a month, and it was going really well. Not only did I enjoy the job, but I met new people every day.

The sun sank closer to the horizon, and I kept walking. Hopefully it wouldn't be completely dark by the time I made it to a house.

Who would I call when I got to a phone? That was limited to the phone numbers I could actually remember. My mom rattled off numbers and amazed us all. But back in her day, speed dial wasn't really a thing.

Lettie was out of town. My sister was too. My boss would probably help me, but I didn't know Tessa's number. Plus, she was probably locking lips with her hot boyfriend in the hot tub. I wouldn't call her.

I'd just have to call a ride share service. Did they even pick up in places this far out of town?

As the sun hovered just above the horizon, I trekked down the road, trying to avoid the puddles left over from yesterday's rain. I wasn't always successful. Walking in a mermaid costume was more difficult than I anticipated, and now I'd have to pay to have this thing cleaned.

Pain stabbed at my ankle, and I swiped at my leg before looking to see what was causing the pain. But then another stab jolted me. This time I looked for the culprit. No! An ant clung to my ankle biting me and stabbing with his butt. Fear rippled through me. I did not need this right now.

In the fading light, I slapped at my ankle and scanned the ground. When I spotted the mound, I jumped away from the ants I'd just disturbed with my tail. Then I noticed them all over my tail. Flicking them off, I turned to make sure they weren't getting on my other leg. Twisting and turning, I fell over and landed with a thud. Stupid mermaid tail. My elbows were scraped up, but at least I hadn't landed in the mud.

Pushing up, I looked around for my purse. Where was it? I needed it.

My skin started to itch, and I made a conscious effort to keep my breathing slow and steady. The panic clawing at my skin didn't help. Why did I have to be allergic to ants? And where was my lobster purse that contained my Epi-pen?

Stupid frat boys.

CHAPTER 2

NICO

*A*fter two days of torrential rains, the clear sky was a welcome sight, and it coincided perfectly with my time off. Tomorrow was supposed to be sunny and glorious, which would be perfect for a day of fishing.

Yawning, I rolled my neck from side to side. Sleeping during the day was never as restful as sleeping at night, but working nights didn't give me much choice. After getting a few hours of shuteye and then running a few errands, I needed dinner.

Best barbecue around was in Stadtburg, and I headed that way.

With the radio blaring, I sang along with Queen, but I didn't quite have the same range.

I did a double take as my headlights lit up something at the edge of the pavement on the opposite side of the road. I knew we'd had a lot of rain yesterday, but enough to wash a mermaid so far inland? That was unlikely.

After easing off the road without getting too close—I didn't want to scare her—I grabbed my flashlight as I jumped out. "Hey. You okay?"

She shook her head.

When I shined the light on her, I understood. She was covered in hives. I didn't bother turning off the flashlight before shoving it in my back pocket and scooping her up.

"Let's get you to a hospital. Just keep breathing for me, all right?" Working in law enforcement, I'd seen a few allergic reactions and knew how serious they could be.

Nodding, she continued intentional breaths. "My purse."

After setting the beautiful stranger in the passenger seat of my truck, I swept the beam of the flashlight along the ground where she'd been sitting. "The lobster?"

"Yes." She started to get out of the truck. "Do you see it?"

"I see it. I think maybe you were sitting on it. I'm coming. Stay put."

She gripped my arm as soon as she could reach me. "I need my Epi-pen."

I dumped the contents of her purse into my back seat and shuffled through Pixie Sticks, feminine products, a plastic frog, and enough hair ties to keep an entire cheerleading squad in ponytails. When I found the Epi-pen, I stepped back to the door.

"Take out that part and jab it into my thigh." She patted her leg.

"But you're wearing—"

"Through my costume. Hurry." Her voice had an edge of panic to it.

For a big guy who wasn't afraid of much, I harbored a horrible fear of needles. Not many people knew about that fear. Trying not to think about the sharp thing poking into her leg, I followed her instructions. When she winced, I could no longer forget the needle part.

Her hand wrapped around mine, keeping the device in place. Hopefully, she could hang on to it if I passed out, which was becoming a real threat. This was a bad time to do that. Blood pooled in my feet, and a wave of lightheadedness hit me. Either I was going to pass out or be sick. Both options were bad. Worse than bad. I needed something to distract me.

The mermaid must have read my thoughts. With her free hand, she grabbed my shirt and pulled me to her lips.

Hello!

My thoughts catapulted in a much different direction. They were now focused on the softest lips I'd ever kissed. I tilted my head and leaned in closer, very much enjoying her surprise distraction.

Little Miss Mermaid shoved on my chest. "Okay, it's been at least eleven seconds. Look away."

"What? Why?"

"Because I don't need you passing out. I need you to drive me to the hospital."

"Got it." I turned around.

A second later, she patted my arm. "What should I do with it? The pokey thing is sticking out."

"Saying pokey thing instead of needle doesn't change anything." I sucked in a deep breath and spun around. "I'll put it back here until I can dispose of it properly."

"Don't look at it." She leaned out of the door, offering unhelpful advice.

"That's like telling someone to calm down. It doesn't work."

I climbed in behind the wheel, feeling rather victorious. I hadn't gotten sick or passed out. After shifting into drive, I glanced at the mermaid. "I'm Nico Gomez. Deputy Nico Gomez, but I'm off duty. What's your name?"

The question was best asked before kissing a woman, but

she held all responsibility for that kiss. I wasn't going to complain about it... except maybe that it was too short. Eleven seconds wasn't nearly long enough.

She smiled and tilted her head back. I guess she didn't want to give me her name.

As we neared the hospital, I reached out my hand.

She clasped my fingers, then slid her hand in mine. "I'm sorry about... you know."

"No need to apologize. And if you feel like doing that again, I'm perfectly okay with it."

Giggling erupted next to me, followed by coughing.

"No laughing for you, lady."

That had the opposite effect. Her hand tightened around mine, and she worked to stop her giggles. "I didn't want you to pass out, so I thought if you had something else to think about. It was just an impulse."

"It worked. And I'll be thinking about it. Guaranteed." I pulled up to the emergency room entrance. "It's not every day I find a mermaid on the side of the road *and* get to kiss her." I ran around to open her door. "I'll move the truck after I get you inside."

"Thank you for rescuing me." She swung her legs out.

I scooped her into my arms. "I'm not sure physics allows for walking in this thing. I'll carry you in."

She leaned her head on my shoulder. "Layla. My name is Layla Tucker."

The nurse, who I knew recognized me from the times I'd dealt with cases here, nodded toward the double doors. "Let me let them know you're coming. Hang on." She didn't even seem fazed that I'd just carried a mermaid into the ER.

Layla kept her head on my shoulder, but her eyes were wide and wild.

"You having trouble breathing?"

She shook her head. "Epinephrine makes me panicky."

I pushed through the double doors. "She's having an allergic reaction to something. I gave her the Epi-pen, and she seemed okay on the drive here, but I'm worried about her."

The nurse pointed at a bed. "Right there, Deputy."

I laid the mermaid down but didn't leave her side.

A doctor rushed in, and the nurse yanked the curtain closed. "I'm Dr. Rios. What's your name?"

"Layla."

"I'm going to look you over really quick. What are you allergic to?"

"Fire ants." Layla reached for my hand.

"Nasty creatures." The doctor listened to her breathing and looked at her hives. "I wish they'd never caught a ride on that cargo ship. Were you at a party?"

She nodded.

"Your airways sound fine. But I'd like to get some Benadryl in you to help ease the hives and itching." He rattled off instructions to the nurse, and they both hurried out of the curtained area.

"Do you live around here?" I hoped a little conversation might help her feel less panicked.

"Stadtburg. I work at the doughnut shop."

"Sweet's?" My day was getting better and better.

She nodded.

"In the rush to get here, I didn't ask about your car."

"Flat tire. Hopefully, it doesn't get towed. I can't afford that." She closed her eyes, her dark hair scattered across the pillow.

The nurse walked in carrying a syringe, and I focused on Layla.

Reminding myself not to look at the needle wasn't working, and when the nurse held up the syringe, the light in the room began to fade. The last thing I heard was my mermaid shouting for someone to catch me.

CHAPTER 3

LAYLA

*I*t took less than fifteen seconds for me to flip my tail over the side of the bed and drop to the floor beside Nico. Leaning over him, I patted his cheek. "Wake up."

He'd hit the arm of the chair on the way down, and that worried me.

After waiting less than a second for a response, I tried something different. If a kiss worked in fairy tales, it was worth a try. For the second time in less than an hour, I kissed the handsome stranger.

He made a noise, and then his hand wrapped around the back of my neck. He'd be fine. And he was fine. Like a tall glass of lemonade on a hot day kind of fine. So, I continued kissing him.

"I need you, Miss Mermaid, on the bed, and you, Deputy Lip Locked, to stay on the floor. Do not even sit up. Y'all can do more of that later when you aren't in the ER."

I ran my fingers through his hair where I guessed he'd gotten whapped. "I need to follow orders. You okay?"

"Better now." He started to pick up his head.

"No. Weren't you listening?" I pulled my hand back, then waved it at the nurse. "He's bleeding."

"That's why I need you out of my way." She seemed greatly displeased.

I climbed back up onto the bed but leaned over the side.

The nurse pointed at me as she knelt beside Nico. "Be careful. I don't need two head injuries."

"I'm okay." Nico waved her away.

"Deputy Gomez, you're bleeding on my floor. That's not okay." She pressed a stack of gauze to the side of his head. "If you can't handle needles, why were you in here?"

"The mermaid." He shot me a glance and grinned.

I might have to write a thank-you note to the frat boys. Or to the person who dropped the board in the road. It probably had a nail in it.

Once the bleeding stopped, which didn't take long, the nurse helped Nico into a chair. "Do *not* get up."

"Ever?" Nico was clearly more interested in my reaction to his attempt at humor.

I laughed.

The nurse rolled her eyes. "The doctor will be in to check on you in a minute, Deputy. Mermaid, I'm going to need you out of the fish tail so I can give you that shot.

Nico pushed on the arms of the chair but dropped back down when he made eye contact with the nurse. "I'll just sit here with my eyes closed."

"Good idea." She rolled her shoulders. "And keep them closed until I tell you to open them."

I stifled a giggle. Nico looked so cute with his eyes squeezed closed.

Mom had always said to make sure that I wore nice undies in case I was in an accident. Every time she'd given me the advice, I'd laughed and ignored it. It had been years since she'd reminded me of that advice, but that advice was what popped in my head. My choice of undergarments had been influenced by theme. Lobster-clad underwear graced my backside. It didn't grace much of it either because I didn't expect anyone to see it.

"Are your eyes closed?" I peeked around the nurse.

Nico nodded and slapped a hand across his face.

I unzipped the costume, then wriggled out of it. Once I had the sheet over me, I reached out and touched the tail to his hand.

He took hold of it without opening his eyes. "I might need a distraction while you give her the shot. Should I—"

The nurse had to be someone's mom, or maybe she had a natural talent for reading minds.

"You should keep your eyes closed. Because if you do that, you won't know anything about the shot." She picked up the syringe and pulled back the sheet.

I stayed super quiet and didn't squeal or moan or even gasp. I should be commended for that because the shot hurt. The nurse adjusted the sheet and covered me just as the doctor walked back in.

"You need to check his head. He passed out because of a fear of needles. Deputy, you can open your eyes now."

The doctor glanced at me. "How are you feeling?"

"Itchy."

"Give the Benadryl time to work." He turned toward Nico and shined a light in his eyes. "You seem okay. Let me see the gash." The doctor moved Nico's hair and pursed his lips. "Hmm."

"Is it bad?" I stretched out my hand to Nico. "I'm so sorry. I should've made you leave."

"Made me?" He gripped my hand. "What's the prognosis, Doc?"

"Nurse Bettis, I think two or three stitches here would do the trick. Will you get that ready for me?"

"Absolutely." She walked toward the curtain, then turned back to face me. "He's going to need a distraction that doesn't involve moving his head."

Dr. Rios looked from Nico to me. "Just focus on her and forget about the—"

"Other stuff." I didn't need my deputy hitting the floor twice in one night.

"Yes. What she said." Chuckling, the doctor walked out. "Be right back."

Nico scooted his chair so that he was facing me. "Would you mind holding my hand? I know it's pretty stupid for me to pass out when thinking about—"

"Kissing me?"

"Right. I'd do that, but I'm not sure I can manage that while being still. Tell me about you." He laced his fingers with mine.

I rolled onto my side. The Benadryl was starting to kick in, and if we didn't get sprung from here soon, I'd need to be carried out. "I moved here last summer. It's been hard meeting new people. Well, making friends. I meet lots of people, and they all seem nice, but…" I shrugged one shoulder. "It seems like everyone here is already married or at least seriously dating. My sister lives here. She's one of the married people."

"She lives in Stadtburg?"

"Near there. She's a teacher at the school, the one across from the hardware store."

"I know the one."

"But two months ago, I met Lettie because she was looking for a roommate. And that's been great. Oh, and I didn't call my sister when I got stuck in the mud because my phone fell into my Dr Pepper. I need to get rice. But even if my phone wasn't out of commission, I wouldn't have called my sister because she's out of town, and even if she was in town, I might not have called her because she hasn't been married that long, and well…"

"I get it." He brushed his thumb along the back of my hand. "How long had you been out there?"

"You pulled up right after I fell. Your timing was… perfect."

He pointed at my elbow. "I missed this."

"It's not that bad." I covered a yawn.

"Your hives are looking a little better. Sleepy?"

"Yeah." I tucked his hand under my cheek.

"As soon as they let us go, I'll drive you home. We'll get your car tomorrow."

I kissed his hand. "Thank you."

Nico squeezed my hand as the nurse rolled in a tray and the doctor wheeled up next to Nico on a stool.

I blew him a kiss. "I met someone today who I hope wants to be my friend."

He smiled, his gaze fixed on mine. "Tell me about your frog."

I'd carried that frog around for three years, and no one had asked about it. Of course he'd pick today to drop that question. "My friend gave it to me as kind of a joke, but only sort of a joke. There is that fairy tale of the princess and the frog."

His smile widened. "Yes?"

"She gave me the frog to remind me that eventually I'd find my prince. I've had it for three years."

"Do you make a habit of kissing frogs?"

"I don't make a habit of kissing anyone. And two times doesn't make something a habit."

His eyebrows lifted. "How many times does it take to become a habit?"

"I'm not sure yet." I truly wanted to make a habit of kissing this wall of a man, the one who swept me off my feet effortlessly and set my heart dancing.

"All done." Dr. Rios rolled away from Nico. "The nurse will put a bandage on that and then y'all can go." He turned to me. "Do you have someone that can stay with you for the next twenty-four hours?"

"Um, well, normally I have a roommate, but she's out of town until later tomorrow." I hated not knowing many people. This meant I'd have to bother Tessa.

Nico stood up. "I'll make sure she isn't alone."

"Good. And you need someone with you too in case you have a mild concussion." Dr. Rios picked up a clipboard off the foot of my bed and scribbled on the papers. "Any questions for me?"

"Can I put my tail back on?"

"Of course. The nurse will be back in with paperwork for you to sign, and then you'll be able to go." He walked out, humming to himself.

Nico handed me the tail, then turned around. "Hurry because if the nurse sees me standing up, she might yell at me again."

I wriggled back into the tail and zipped up the side. "I'm decent."

"I'd say you are way better than decent. I'd give those kisses at least an eight." His dark eyes twinkled with mischief.

"I'll have to do better next time." This kind of impulsive flirting was how I ended up making bad choices.

He clasped my hand again. "I know we've only just met, but if you'll let me, I'd like to stay with you tonight. I don't mean *with* you, but because the doctor said—"

"Nico, I know what you mean. And I'd feel horrible leaving you alone after you've done so much for me. Your place or mine?"

He nodded toward my tail. "I'm guessing you'll probably want to change clothes."

"Yes, but I can pick stuff up. Besides, I'm not sure you'll fit on my couch."

"I have that problem." Nico dropped back into the chair as the nurse walked in. "Mine is L-shaped with recliners at both ends. Plenty big."

The nurse put her hands on her hips, a clipboard sticking out on each side. "Y'all are quite a pair. And, silly me, I thought tonight would be quiet and uneventful." She handed us each a clipboard. "Sign these, and then y'all can resume your kissing elsewhere."

That lady was not helping me curb my impulsive ways.

CHAPTER 4

NICO

I watched my feet as I followed Layla to her apartment, careful not to step on the fin swishing back and forth behind her. The tail served as a helpful distraction from staring at the rest of her. The woman was wearing a fish tail and a bikini top.

When we arrived at the door, she dug around in her purse for her keys. While she searched her purse, I had visions of the keys being lost in my truck from when I'd dumped out the contents in the back seat. Or worse, lost along the side of the road.

She held them up and jingled the keys. "Found 'em."

The keychain had a frog on it. She really had a thing for frogs.

We hadn't been upright next to each other much since we'd met, and standing here as she unlocked the door, our height difference was obvious. She had to be at least a foot shorter than me. Probably more than that.

The door swung open, and before I could ask if she wanted me to wait outside, she clasped my hand and tugged me inside. "I shouldn't be long. You won't care if I wear pajamas on the way to your place, right? I don't see the point of putting on regular clothes and then changing again when I get to your place."

"Don't mind a bit." I maintained eye contact with her and didn't let my gaze wander.

"Good. Okay. Be right back." She held up a finger, then spun and waddled down the hall.

I rubbed my face and paced. What a night. No one was going to believe this story. I still wasn't sure if I'd wake up in the morning and realize it was all a dream. That was the upside to staying together tonight. I'd know first thing in the morning. Then I could either ask her out or find a therapist. If I was having realistic dreams about mermaids, frogs, and my fear of needles, I probably needed to talk that through with a professional.

She rubbed my back as she stepped around me. Then, as natural as anything she slid her hands up my chest and around my neck, lifting the hem of her sweatshirt above her waistline. The waistband of her pajama pants—pants made of hot pink fabric covered in bright green frogs—was rolled over at least twice. The fin fit her better than her pajamas. And to get her arms around my neck, she was on her tiptoes.

"More comfortable?" I wrapped my arms around her.

She nodded. "I'm not really superstitious or anything, but numbers matter to me. I have this thing about odd numbers being lucky."

I didn't have the slightest clue where she was headed with this train of thought. And as long as she was pressed against me, chatting away, I didn't care that I didn't have a clue. "Okay."

"And when I'm at your place, I don't think I should..." She

blew out a breath, then dropped her forehead to my chest. "No kissing once we get to your place. Or anything else. Because I'm far too infatuated to make wise decisions right now."

"Too infatuated, huh?" I inhaled the fruity scent of her shampoo as I whispered in her ear.

"That was probably way too honest."

"Not at all. And I'm fine with your wishes. I understand." I still had no clue how odd numbers and not kissing fit together, so I didn't fully understand. But the boundary issues were clear, and I'd respect those.

"Okay, good. So, will you kiss me now?"

She didn't have to ask twice for a third kiss. I bent down and touched my lips to hers, making her odd-numbered dreams come true. Without breaking our kiss, I scooped her into my arms, and she giggled. What a sound. This had to be a dream, but I intended to enjoy every last second until I woke up.

* * *

I UNLOCKED my front door and pushed it open for Layla to enter first. "Make yourself at home. It's kind of a mess because I wasn't expecting company."

Chewing her bottom lip, she stepped inside and glanced around. "Nice place."

As much as I wanted to chew on that bottom lip for her, I wouldn't. Not because it was obvious she was nervous and sleepy, but because she'd been clear about what she didn't want.

I liked a woman who knew what she wanted. "If you want to talk to someone who can vouch for me, I can arrange that. Tessa would. Probably. We sort of got off to a rough start because—yeah. Never mind all that. Garrett would vouch for me. I swear you're safe here."

Smiling, she positioned herself right in front of me and rested one hand on my chest. "I already decided that I trust you. It's kind of like when you see a really gorgeous book cover, and you know you'll love the story." Nodding toward the couch, she covered a yawn before speaking again. "Can I sleep here?"

If her analogy meant that she thought I was gorgeous, I'd happily stick around for the second part. I really needed to get my head in reality and out of fairy-tale land. "Yeah. Since we're supposed to watch out for each other, I figured, I'd sleep here in this recliner."

She curled up in the spot next to it. "Okay."

I ran back to my room and grabbed pillows and blankets. "Here. Use this." Once she'd tucked the pillow under her head, I draped a blanket over her. "If you need anything, tap me."

"Okay." Her voice sounded dreamy and far away.

"I'm going to run back and change." I lingered a second, studying her as she lay there with her eyes closed.

She wasn't the only one with a case of infatuation.

After changing into something appropriate for our little sleepover, I settled into the recliner and pulled a blanket over me. Gently, I ran my fingers through her hair.

She was adorable in a curvy, pint-sized package. With a hand on her shoulder, I tilted my head back and closed my eyes, waiting for the sleep fairies to visit.

Layla bolted upright. "Where's my phone? How long have you been asleep?" She seemed to like saying things that didn't fit together.

"Your phone is in the tub of rice on the coffee table. And I haven't fallen asleep yet."

"We need to set an alarm to wake you every two hours. Isn't that what the nurse said?"

It was possible, but I didn't remember that part. My brain had been more focused on other parts the evening. "Maybe. Don't remember."

"Will you set yours?"

"Sure." I set an alarm to go off every two hours, then put the phone where she could reach it.

When she lay back down, she shifted the pillow so that her head bumped against my thigh. "Your hand is warm. It feels nice." She sighed with contentment and laced her fingers with mine.

Holding hands with her, I closed my eyes and enjoyed the dream. If this whole night had been a fabrication of my mind, it was about to end. Waking always followed sleep, but I wasn't ready to wake up from this dream.

CHAPTER 5

LAYLA

$\mathcal{I}$ dismissed the alarm and closed my eyes. Perfectly comfortable, I didn't want to get up, but I had to. I'd skipped the last wakeup alarm because Nico had clearly been breathing. But after so many hours, I really needed to check on him.

Yawning, I poked his leg. "You okay?"

He didn't answer.

I sat up. "Nico?"

His head was tilted back, and his mouth was open, but he wasn't snoring. Didn't all guys snore? It wasn't like I'd ever spent the night with one before.

I climbed on top of him, straddling his lap. Then I patted his cheek. "Nico, please wake up."

One eye opened, then closed again. "Hey."

"Oh, thank goodness. You aren't dead." I trailed a finger through his stubble. "I was a little worried when you didn't wake up."

"Remember what you said about not kissing?" His eyes were still closed as he talked.

I was determined not to break that boundary no matter how much I wanted to. If this was more than a passing flirtation, there would be time later for more kisses. "What about it?"

He stretched, then rested his hands on my hips. "It'll be a lot easier if you aren't in my lap."

I really hadn't thought that one through. "Sorry." I scrambled off him and sat next to him. "I just wanted you to wake up."

"Oh, I'm awake." He turned to face me, his head still tilted back. "Good morning. I don't think I've ever been so happy to realize something wasn't a dream."

"I'm not a figment of your imagination. And you aren't a figment of mine. I don't think I could've even dreamed up anyone like you." Why did I keep saying whatever popped into my head?

He brushed a knuckle across my cheek. "Since the rule is no kissing at my house, why don't I take you to breakfast?"

I giggled, then slapped a hand over my mouth. Holding my breath, I waited until the funny tickle that set me giggling calmed down.

"What?"

"I was trying not to giggle. I've been told that it's annoying, and I'm trying to stop. But I thought the idea of going to breakfast in my pajamas was funny. I mean, I'm not even wearing a—" I clamped my mouth shut.

"I'll take you to breakfast in your pajamas. I don't care what you wear. And I love the sunshine of your giggle. It's not annoying. Whoever said that was wrong." He crossed his arms. "There aren't many things that can make me smile before coffee, but that sound is on the short list."

"I've heard it from more than one person, so I thought..."

I'd spent a lot of time trying to be different and reminding myself to curb my natural impulses. Moving to Stadtburg had been an attempt to start over as someone different. I just wasn't very good at being someone else.

"They're all wrong. And if you'll give me a list of names, I'll visit them personally and explain that to them." He ran his thumb across my bottom lip. "More than explain if necessary."

Imagining Nico running around to all the people who'd told me my giggling was annoying and made me sound like an airhead set off my giggles.

He grinned. "Too much?"

"Just right." I hugged him. "Let me shower and change super quick." After picking up my bag, I ran down the hall. I probably should've waited to hug him until after I'd changed and was in more than a baggy sweatshirt and pajama pants.

He'd set stuff out in the bathroom so that I had everything I needed. I'd fallen asleep hard last night.

After a quick shower, I stepped out of the bathroom fully dressed and smelling like a guy. That was better than being stinky.

The living room was empty, so I wandered through that room and kitchen, getting a sense of who this Nico guy really was.

There were dirty dishes in the sink, but the table was clean. Notes covered the freezer door, held there by an assortment of magnets. He didn't seem like the sort of guy to collect magnets. The couch had no throw pillows. Three remotes were scattered on the coffee table beside a game controller.

I used the few minutes to wash off the dishes and load them into the dishwasher. When I heard a door open, I ran to the hall.

Nico was walking up the hall, pulling a T-shirt down over his head. That chest looked as good as it felt.

I sighed inadvertently, and he froze as he worked the shirt down the rest of the way.

"Sorry. I didn't realize you were right there. There was sound coming from the kitchen, and I thought..."

"I'm the one who should apologize for sneaking up on you, but I'm not sorry about it." I spun around to go make sure I had all my stuff. "I'm ready whenever you are."

Nico slipped his arms around me from behind. How could a guy built like a wall sneak up on someone? "Are you a steak and eggs breakfast or a doughnut and coffee sort of person?"

I leaned back into his embrace. "Steak and eggs with coffee. Always coffee."

"The more I learn about you, the more I like you." He picked up my bag. "Let's go eat."

My misadventure in a mermaid costume had turned into one of the best mornings ever. I smiled up at my hunk, then reminded myself to slow down. I didn't know him well. What if all the nice things he'd said were just lines? It wouldn't be the first time a guy had said things just to win my attention. But those guys all changed their tune after a short time.

How long would it take to figure out if Nico really liked my giggling or if he was just feeding me a line?

CHAPTER 6

NICO

When we arrived at the restaurant, I ran around and opened Layla's door.

"Thanks." She climbed out and crossed her arms, tucking her hands out of sight.

A waitress waved as we walked in. "Sit anywhere."

Layla stepped behind me. "I'll follow you."

I chose a booth in the corner, then waited to sit until she'd slid onto the bench. "Are you still itching?"

She shook her head. "The hives have all disappeared. How's your head?"

"Fine. It only hurts if I push on the bump."

"Then don't." She giggled, then pinched her lips together.

The irritation with the people who'd convinced her that she needed to change had my insides roiling. It was now my mission to encourage her to be herself.

"Wise woman. I think I'll follow that advice."

If I let my emotions rule me now, I'd probably mess this up. The carefree woman from yesterday had been replaced with a more reserved version, someone who was filtering every thought and word. Shoot, it was the woman from yesterday who'd woken me up this morning, but somewhere between here and the house, her demeanor had changed.

She smiled as the waitress walked up to the table. "Good morning."

"Morning. Here are menus. What can I get y'all to drink?"

The waitress barely had the last word out before Layla said, "Coffee."

"Cream and sugar?"

Layla shook her head. "Just black."

"Same for me." I opened my menu, my gaze still locked on her.

"I'll have those out in a moment." The waitress hurried away from the table.

Layla picked up her menu, and it blocked my view of her face. But when I lifted mine, her menu dropped a little.

"Have you figured out what you want?"

Her eyes widened. "Huh? No. I mean, we only just—" She glanced down at the menu. "Oh, you're talking about breakfast."

At least now I didn't have to wonder what was occupying her thoughts, but I had an awful feeling in my gut that I wouldn't like the way today ended. Until then, I'd do my best to build that friendship she'd mentioned yesterday.

"I was, but if you'd rather talk about something else, I'm all ears."

"No. I'm having the steak and eggs." She closed the menu and shoved it toward the end of the table. "Did you grow up around here?"

"San Antonio. My family is still there, but I found a job

out here." I set my menu on top of hers. "I have a cousin who lives around here. He's a ranch hand out at Stargazer Springs Ranch."

"Why don't you live in Stadtburg?"

"I live in the county where I work. Stadtburg isn't in that county. I found that house to rent, and I like living in the middle of nowhere." After growing up in a city, sleeping with the windows open and not hearing street noises was a nice change. And the stars were brighter without all the lights polluting the sky. "What about you? Where did you move from?"

She opened her mouth, but before she could speak, I grabbed her hand.

"Wait. Let me guess." When she glanced down at my hand, I let go. "I figure you're from Texas by the way you sound, so…" I pursed my lips and cocked my head, acting like I was thinking hard. "San Marcos."

Her jaw fell open. "How did you…"

"It's the Mermaid Capitol of Texas." I was as stunned as she was. I was trying to be funny, but I turned out to be right. That combination—funny and right—rarely happened.

Coffee mugs appeared on the table, and the waitress smiled. "Have you decided?"

I nodded for Layla to go first.

"I'll take the ribeye and eggs."

The waitress scribbled on her little pad. "What side?"

"Hashbrowns."

"And how do you want your steak?"

"Medium rare."

"Your eggs?"

Layla's brow pinched. "Um, over easy."

The waitress looked at me. "For you?"

"The same."

"Y'all are making this easy." She winked and wandered back through the tables, checking on customers as she made her way to the kitchen.

Layla crossed her arms. "I appreciate everything you've done. And I'm sorry I…" She stared into her coffee cup. "I don't always think through things before I do them. I'm impulsive, so I'm sorry for kissing you and climbing on you, and other stuff I probably did and can't remember right now."

"I didn't mind a bit." I shifted, using the delay to choose my words. "Would you be interested in going out with me Saturday night?" Since it was only Monday, waiting until Saturday felt like a long time, but I didn't want to rush things.

She pinched her lips together. "My roommate got back in town early, so after we eat, if you'll take me home, she can help me get my car."

I didn't like the idea of her changing a tire on that road. "I texted a buddy of mine this morning, and he's fixing the tire and driving your car to your apartment. As a favor." The change of subject was enough of an answer to my other question. My gut was right.

"He'll need my keys."

"And you handed me the keys last night."

"Oh." She curled the corner of her napkin, then smoothed it back out. "Can I think about Saturday?" Her lower lip was between her teeth again.

"Sure."

She leaned back as our waitress set our food on the table, and when it was just us again, she touched my hand as I reached for my silverware. "I've pinched myself so many times I think I'm going to have a bruise. I've been working on curbing my impulsiveness, and saying yes to you—this whole thing—is just one impulsive explosion of attraction."

"I get that. Friends, then?"

Her head bobbed up and down. "I hope so."

I did too. As soon as I dropped her off, I planned to call Garrett. If anyone was an expert on navigating the friend zone, it was that man.

CHAPTER 7

LAYLA

I flopped across the bed and hugged my pillow. "Am I an idiot for not saying yes?"

Lettie clicked her tongue. "I'm not sure I understand why you didn't. If he likes your giggling, why is that a problem?"

"No one ever really likes my giggling. Guys say they do, but then after the first date, they ghost me or they hang around waiting for me to sleep with them, and when I won't, the giggling becomes irritating. I don't have enough fingers to count the times a guy has said he thinks my giggling is adorable only to change his mind shortly after." I burrowed my face in my pink pillow and sighed. "And I like this one. A lot."

"Because he's tall?" Lettie rolled her eyes, but her smile gave away her teasing.

She was eight inches taller than me and gave me a hard time about dating guys so tall.

"I can't help what I like. And honestly, even if he were

short, I might like him. He's funny… and cute. That dark hair. And dark eyes but with a twinkle. He asked about my frog."

"Prince Nicolaus, the charming amphibian just waiting to morph into perfection."

I tossed a pillow at her. "The name is a coincidence. We named that frog years ago. Please. You can't tell him."

"Why would I tell him? That's something he should hear from you." She put a hand to her chest and fluttered her eyelashes. "It's like a fairy tale."

"Stop. I should never have kissed him."

"I think you're worrying too much. See what happens. If he keeps showing up, you could give him a chance." She lay down next to me. "Those other guys were nuts. Your giggle is fun. Plus, you're gorgeous."

While I appreciated the compliment, I wasn't great at handling people saying nice things about me, so I found a new topic. "Have you talked to your cowboy?"

"I haven't worked up the nerve to contact him. He probably doesn't want to see me."

"Then moving here was a great plan. You realize this is a small town, right?" I whapped her with the pillow. "You should at least talk to him."

"Maybe. Probably. I'll think about it." She rolled to her back and covered her face. "I was hoping to lose ten or twenty pounds before seeing him again, but that'll take me a year or more."

"If he doesn't like you now, it doesn't matter what he thinks of you twenty pounds lighter." I rubbed her shoulder. "Give him a chance."

Rolling her head to face me, she grinned. "That's great advice."

"The give him a chance part?"

"Nope. The other part." She stood up and pointed at me. "If he doesn't like the giggly, impulsive Layla, it doesn't matter what he thinks of the person you are pretending to be."

"How rude! You are using my own words against me."

She curtsied. "My job here is done. I'm headed to bed. Four comes early."

I hadn't even given Nico my number, but he knew where I lived. If he sought me out, then I'd give him a chance. Rolling onto my stomach, I sighed into my pillow again. Why had I kissed him? More than once!

I'd set the wrong expectation from the outset. Even if he did show up one day, the chance I'd give him would be narrow. No kissing. At least in the beginning.

* * *

THE SHOP WAS extra busy for a Tuesday morning, but I enjoyed the busy days. For one, I felt like I was needed, and the day went by more quickly.

The door opened, and I froze when Tessa spoke. "Welcome to Sweet's—Nico, hi!"

He came. It hadn't even been twenty-four hours since I'd seen him, but here he was in the doughnut shop. Duh. The doughnut shop. He was here for a doughnut. I tamped down my excitement, but my brain didn't get the memo to my cheeks. They were probably flaming pink.

I stared at the counter, trying to breathe normally. Hugging would lead to kissing. I'd learned that from past experience—not with him—but in general. Knowing that, I didn't run around the counter to greet him.

"Good morning." He leaned down to catch my eye. "How are you today?"

"Really good. Thank you." I didn't have to lie about that,

but I reminded myself that he was here for a doughnut. "What can I get you?"

"I'll think about it, but I wanted to run an idea by you."

"An idea?" I glanced around Nico when the door opened, then focused on him again.

Garrett wasn't here to see me, and if he needed a doughnut, Tessa would get it for him. I knew that routine.

"What idea?" I held my breath, hoping this one chance wouldn't be ruined by an idea I'd hate.

Nico folded his arms and rested them on the counter, putting us at eye level. "I did a little research, and while there are differing answers, it seems a habit can be formed in twenty-one days. One person said as few as eighteen days, but for this to work, I really wanted an odd number."

"Okay?" Usually, I was the one confusing people, but right now, I had no clue where he was headed with this idea.

A hush fell over the room, and I saw Garrett on one knee. Tapping Nico's arm, I pointed.

He spun around and leaned back against the counter.

As much as I wanted to watch Tessa say yes, Nico's back was a distraction. The seams at the shoulders were taut, and I could tell there were muscles there even with his shirt on. He had carried me around like I weighed nothing yesterday, so yeah. He had muscles. I think even his muscles had muscles.

Tessa threw her arms around Garrett, and we all cheered. It wasn't a surprise that she'd said yes. I'd only known her a month, and it was clear she was just as smitten with Garrett as he was with her.

I smiled and waved as Garrett carried her out of the shop. "I've got this! Have fun." It was a good thing I was here. Today, I felt needed.

Nico turned back around. "That was sweet."

"Very romantic." I held up a mug and a to-go cup. "Which do you need?"

"Since you're working until the place closes, I'm definitely going to need a mug." He perched on the stool nearest the register after getting himself coffee. "Back to my idea. Supposing I wanted to make a habit of talking to you every day, would that idea appeal to you?"

"Only *talking*?" No one had ever asked me just to talk.

He nodded, then sipped his black coffee. "We'll work on one habit at a time."

"I like that idea."

"Then I'm going to need your number." He slid his phone across the counter with a contact already created for The Mermaid.

I giggled. "You seriously set up my contact like that?"

That twinkle was back in his eyes. "I was hoping it would earn me at least a tiny giggle."

For the next hour, Nico sat on that stool, sipping coffee. When it wasn't busy, we chatted about childhood pets, places we'd like to visit, and whether cheese or toppings should be on the top of a pizza.

They were called toppings for a reason, but he didn't agree.

Nico stood and stretched. He'd never ordered a doughnut, and I guessed that was on purpose to make a point. He'd shown up to see me.

"I'll talk to you later. Should we count today as day one?"

"Today is day three." I laid my hand on his. "I think I'm going to like this habit."

"That makes two of us." He sauntered out of the shop, looking very prince-like.

CHAPTER 8

NICO

 I'd managed a few hours of sleep, and even that was a surprise. Garrett's advice had been simple, but helpful—Build trust and a friendship while making it obvious you're interested. I could do that because I was definitely interested, and not just because she'd kissed me within minutes of our meeting.

Having Garrett propose in the middle of my suggestion to Layla hadn't been planned, but it set the right tone. Serendipity.

The look on her face when she'd clarified that I was only asking for talking amused me. She'd probably been asked out a lot but never asked to only talk.

Before pulling out of my driveway, I dialed her number and put it on speaker.

"Hello." Her greeting was hesitant.

Probably because she had no idea who was calling. I'd

gotten her number, but I hadn't given her mine. "Hi. It's Nico."

"Oh, hi!"

If her greeting was anything like that for the rest of our habit-building days, I'd be smiling for sure. "I'm headed to work and thought I'd chat with you for a bit before my shift starts."

"Do you always work nights?"

"Alternating months. That's the way this county schedules deputies." For some women, dating a deputy was a deal breaker. I hoped that wasn't true for Layla, but I understood how some could be concerned.

"What time does your shift end? Will you text me when you get off tomorrow so that I know your night went okay?"

"Maybe I'll even make a quick detour by the shop after seven. But yes, I'll text you."

She was quiet, and I imagined her chewing that bottom lip.

That image could be very distracting. I needed to file that away until I was done with my shift. "You still there?"

"I'm here. Just to clarify the rules of this habit—does texting count as talking?"

"Do mermaids live in the desert?"

She giggled. "I guess that means no."

"Hearing your voice is my reward for completing my daily task. I researched habits. There has to be a reward for it to work well." And on my personal score card, I got a gold star every time she giggled because of something I said.

The quiet was my cue to move onto a different topic, something less uncomfortable for her.

"I was talking to my cousin just before I left the house. There was a wedding on the ranch this evening."

She gasped. "No way! Garrett didn't waste any time."

"He did not." I had a pretty good idea of where they might

be spending their honeymoon, but I didn't plan on sharing that information with anyone. "I'm sure news will spread quickly, and I figured you'd want to know."

I pulled into the parking lot, not ready to end the call.

"So, you're in uniform?"

"Yep." I leaned back in my seat, reminding myself I'd only known her since Sunday evening and that she hadn't seen me in my work clothes. "What all deputies wear: uniform, boots, and a hat."

The sigh from the other end of the line, which I guessed wasn't supposed to be loud enough for me to hear, made my night. I'd definitely be stopping for doughnuts in the morning. In uniform.

"Are you at the station?"

"I am. Just parked." But I wasn't in much of a hurry to get out of my truck even though my shift started soon.

"I'll let you go then. Thanks for calling me."

"The pleasure was all mine, Layla." I pocketed my keys. "I'll talk to you tomorrow."

"I'm looking forward to it."

Once my shift ended, I'd stop somewhere and buy a wall calendar. What was happening with Layla was worth marking off the days.

Getting my thoughts focused on work, I walked into the station and nearly ran into Edward.

He patted my shoulder. "Must've been a good fishing trip."

"What are you talking about?"

"I heard you caught a mermaid. That has to be one whopper of a story." Edward Bettis laughed. "One I'd really like to hear."

"Nothing to tell. And what happened to medical privacy?" I rolled my eyes and kept walking.

He kept pace. "My mom mentioned that you'd walked in carrying a mermaid. There is nothing medical about that."

"I suppose. Yes, I carried a mermaid into the hospital on Sunday night. Happy?"

He laughed. "I'll leave you alone. For now."

I didn't want to think about what else his mom might've told him. Living in a small town had its perks and downfalls. This was definitely the latter.

My phone rang, and I strode to the end of the hall before answering. "Hello."

"Nico, it's Brian. Just wanted to make sure all was good with the car. Did my guys get it delivered without issue?"

"They did. Thank you so much."

"I owed you. Speaking of that, my girlfriend's cousin is coming back to town. Any chance you'd take her out again? Double date. I'll pay for everything."

"Sorry. Can't do that."

"I'll throw in a free oil change." Brian sounded a little desperate.

I felt for the man, but that wouldn't change my answer. "Not this time. I'm sure you can find someone else to round out the double date."

"She's taller than me, and she doesn't date short guys. You're the only one I know who fits her criteria." He sighed. "But I won't pester you. If you change your mind, let me know."

"Thanks for getting the car."

"No problem." Brian ended the call, and I hurried into the meeting room for the shift briefing.

I leaned against the wall in the back, trying to think of someone else who would be willing to help Brian out. In the morning, I'd give my cousin a call. Maybe Dag would do it. He was as tall as me, and women liked him. He was a bit older, but that probably wouldn't matter.

The captain walked in, and everyone quieted. All thoughts of dates and Layla were boxed up and put away.

I was now on duty.

CHAPTER 9

LAYLA

𝓘 walked from table to table, checking on customers. The first hour of business had flown by, but now that it was after seven, every time the door opened and a burst of air swooped into the shop, I glanced over to see who was walking in. Not because I wanted to welcome customers but because I wanted it to be Nico walking through the door. I'd spent half the night dreaming about how he'd look in uniform.

There were so many things about him I liked. He was tall and strong, which on my attraction scale rated him about fifteen out of ten. He had warm hands, which weren't small. And even just the memory of those dark eyes set my heart fluttering.

But what had really won me over wasn't his looks. And it wasn't his kindness, even though he'd been very kind. What had me swooning was how he'd taken what felt like rushing water and calmed it. When he'd asked me out at the restaurant, I felt head over heels and discombobulated. Feeling out of control bothered me. But Nico changed all that.

His actions signaled he was interested in more than a quick fling. That was what had my heart doing back flips.

The best part was while I was excited about seeing him and talking to him, I didn't feel dragged along by my emotions or the chemistry sparking between us.

Lettie called out from the kitchen that she had another batch of doughnuts ready, and I ran back behind the counter to load up the display case. It was good that Lettie had made extra today. We were busier than normal with people who wanted a doughnut and the scoop on Tessa and Garrett.

The door opened again, and a group of firefighters walked in. One of the guys veered away from the counter and lifted a woman off the ground, kissing her until the people around them laughed. I needed to get better with names. That was one of Tessa's friends, and I was pretty sure she worked at the photography studio next door.

She and her husband were kissing almost every time I saw them together. Part of me was a wee bit jealous. Not of her husband, but of that type of relationship. In the month I'd worked here, I'd noticed them because the woman giggled. And when she did, her husband looked at her like she hung the moon. Honestly, he always looked at her that way. It was sweet.

The door opened again, and I whipped around, a smile at the ready. A middle-aged cowboy, who was built like Nico strolled in, holding hands with a woman shorter than me. They wandered up to the counter, and he stepped behind her, wrapping his arms around her. "What do you want, Joji? The usual?"

How sweet was it that he knew her usual? I'd seen her in before but never with him. With the height difference and the overall cuteness, they were my new favorite couple.

"Good morning, what can I get y'all?"

Joji leaned forward. "I'm so glad Tessa found you. She's off happily enjoying her honeymoon, and I still get a doughnut."

The tall cowboy patted her hip. "We're both happy about the doughnut part."

They ordered coffee and doughnuts, and I handed over their goodies. "Let me know if you need anything else."

Joji grabbed her man's hand. "Will do. But I think I have everything I need right here. Right, Clint?"

He nodded, a satisfied grin on his face.

The air changed in the room, and I glanced at the door. It was an older couple who, based on his scrunched-up face and her sour expression, seemed to be in the middle of a squabble. They sat at the table closest to the door without coming to the counter first, which wasn't typical, but not exactly weird.

After giving them a minute, I walked by the table, headed to the coffee station. "Good morning." I wiped up spilled sugar and drips of coffee. "The coffee is fresh. I just made a new pot."

The man looked over his shoulder at me. "Sounds like just what I need. I'll get some in a minute."

The woman, who was presumably his wife, rolled her eyes but didn't say anything. Not all couples made me jealous of what they had.

The door opened again, and my heart fluttered to a stop. My dreams didn't even compare with reality. Nico grinned as he pulled the cowboy hat off his head. Like a dork, I fanned myself with a coffee cup sleeve.

He let the door close behind him and stepped toward me. "Hey."

"I like your..." I glanced at the table with the bickering

couple as the wife's voice broke through the spell of my romantic slow-mo moment.

Her voice was shrill. "Just stick the needle in already. I don't know why you didn't just poke yourself in the car. No one cares if you lift your shirt a little. Just jab it in."

I looked over, and the man had a needle aimed at his stomach. Hoping to distract Nico, I ran up to him, but it was too late. His gaze cut to the couple, and then his eyes rolled back.

I pressed my hands to his chest, determined to hold him up. "I've got you."

In my head, I envisioned the two of us crumpling to the floor gently, and Nico landing in my arms. Reality was much different and more painful. His knees buckled, we sank to the floor, and then I toppled backward. We landed in a tangled heap with him on top. I didn't even know where his hands were.

"I don't got you." I pushed on his chest, needing him to move so I wasn't so squished. "Hey there, cuddle bug, could you shift a bit?"

His eyelids fluttered, and I noticed how long his lashes were. How was it fair that a guy had lashes that amazing?

"Nico." I was pretty much whispering into his chest, then looked up and met Lettie's gaze.

"You okay?" She held her phone at the ready.

"Mostly. Just keep people back." I slid my hand up to Nico's neck, and that sparked movement.

His fingers wiggled against the only ticklish spot on my body, right along my waist. Calling it one spot bordered on deceptive because I was ticklish all the way around from the middle of my ribs down to my hips. And his hands—one of them at least—were touching this region. And there wasn't a shirt between my skin and his fingers.

I tensed until he moved again. Then my giggles exploded.

With his eyes still closed, he smiled, and his fingers moved even more.

"Please stop. I can barely breathe."

In an instant, Nico shoved up and braced himself on his elbows. There was no longer a smile on his face. "I'm so sorry." His words were wrapped in agony and tied up with a bow of disappointment.

I slipped my hands around his neck and pulled myself up to whisper in his ear. "The next time we cuddle and talk, I suggest we don't do it on the floor of the doughnut shop. And I want to be on top."

His breath caught, and he was still for a few heartbeats. Then he shifted and whispered in my ear. "Want to get together and talk before my shift tonight?"

His response tickled almost as much as his fingers had, and I giggled. Loudly. I eased myself back to the floor, and when I saw the smolder in Nico's expression, my giggling stopped.

I'd never been more thankful for Lettie and her ability to control a crowd, a talent I didn't know she had.

His gaze bounced between my eyes and my lips, then settled on my eyes. "Only talking."

"Yeah."

He shifted as if he was about to get up.

I locked my arms around his neck. "The nurse didn't want you to get up right away. Stay down a minute."

He glanced around.

"Forget about the people. Look at me." I trailed a finger along his collar. "Now I get why some women have a thing for guys in uniform."

Blinking, he pulled in a deep breath. "This is embarrassing."

"I have a whole list of embarrassing stories. If you stick around, maybe I'll share them sometime."

The haze in his eyes cleared, and the previous smolder turned into an inferno. "I absolutely plan to stick around."

Whoa! I was not prepared for that look. I shifted to a sitting position beside him. With the looks he was giving me, I was at risk of embarrassing myself in front of the entire shop. And I liked my job.

I patted his chest. "Let's see if you can get up. But maybe you should rest your head on the counter for a bit."

"I'm fine." With the flexibility and agility surprising for someone built like a wall, he was on his feet in a second, then extended his hand to me.

Everyone in the shop clapped, which wasn't helpful.

Nico waved, the tips of his ears a bright red.

Once I was on my feet, I snaked an arm around his waist. "Aren't you supposed to be careful or sit down or something?"

"I'm okay. But a doughnut would help me feel better." He leaned into me, betraying that he wasn't quite fully recovered.

I hugged him again. "Whatever you want."

I meant it in regard to doughnuts, but part of me meant it in so many other ways. I'd known him only a few days, but he'd been clear about what he wanted. It both thrilled me and scared me that he was interested in me.

Holding onto him, I made sure he was seated on his favorite stool. "Please sit for a bit. Please."

He nodded. "For you."

The old man trudged up and rested a hand on Nico's arm. "Forgive me. I've been giving myself—"

I shook my head.

The man nodded. "I've been giving myself medicine for so long, I don't even think about it. And I'm sorry."

Nico shook the man's hand. "You didn't do anything wrong."

The wife, on the other hand, should learn to keep her voice down. No one would have been the wiser if she hadn't announced it to the room.

"Thank you." The man walked back toward his table.

I rubbed Nico's arm. "Decaf?"

"Probably a good idea."

After setting a mug of coffee in front of him, I pointed at the display case. "What'll it be?"

"Snickerdoodle."

I set one on a plate and handed it to him.

"I really am sorry. Not only was that embarrassing, but I hurt you."

I tugged up the collar of my shirt before leaning over the counter. If I could get through the day without a peep show, that would be good. "I'm okay, and don't be embarrassed. Every hero needs a weakness."

THAT AFTERNOON as I slipped off my apron, four small plastic frogs fell out of the pocket. I didn't even remember picking them up. It had been busy, but I didn't think it had been busy enough to make me forget things. I set the four little frogs next to the register, figuring if they were dearly missed, a mom would be back to pick them up one day.

CHAPTER 10

NICO

Friday night, I glanced at my phone as I hurried to the front door. I wasn't sure who was knocking at my door, but I planned to get rid of them quickly so I could stay on schedule. With only an hour and a half until I went on shift, time with Layla would be limited as it was. I hadn't even planned for dinner, but I'd figure it out. I wasn't in danger of starving.

I'd stopped by Layla's before going on shift every night this week, and while it took a bit of juggling to make the schedule work, it was worth it. Tonight, I'd overslept a bit, which was why I was answering my door wearing only gray sweatpants and drying my hair.

I pulled open the door. "Layla?"

With that bottom lip between her teeth, she grinned as her gaze slowly moved from my bare chest to my face. She held out a pan covered in foil. "I brought dinner."

"I thought I was going to your place."

"Is this a problem?" Whatever she carried into the kitchen smelled amazing.

I tossed the towel over my shoulder. "Not at all. It's a nice surprise."

She'd changed out of the slacks and shirt she'd had on earlier and was now in leggings and a baggy sweatshirt. I tried not to think about whatever else she was or wasn't wearing.

"It's just a simple dinner. Lettie is definitely better in the kitchen than I am, but she wasn't around this afternoon. It's homemade mac and cheese with sausage added." She set the dish on the counter and stared at the calendar on the wall. Blinking, she slowly spun around. "Are you marking off the days…"

"I take habit-building seriously. See the day outlined in red. That's day twenty-one." I stepped closer to her. "As for the pictures, who doesn't want to look at wildflowers?"

Her gaze swept the kitchen, paused at my chest, then moved to the fridge. "Are those all your magnets or did you get them from someone else?"

"When I graduated from college, I took a road trip, and every place I stopped, I bought a magnet."

Her shoulder brushed against me as she walked to the fridge. "Looks like it was a fun trip."

"It was. Do you like road trips?"

"Never been on one." She cocked her head. "I've been thinking, and if the offer for Saturday still stands, I'd be interested. I know it's short notice."

"It absolutely still stands." I hadn't expected that topic to come up again, but I wasn't complaining that it did. "Dinner and dancing?"

"Two steppin'?" Her eyes sparkled.

"Yes, ma'am. And talking." The smell of the food was

making me hungry, and my stomach announced that to the room.

Layla giggled. "We should probably eat."

"Let me grab a shirt." I chuckled as she sighed behind me.

I hadn't pressed her to label what this was. My interest wasn't hidden, and having her bring up Saturday confirmed that I wasn't crazy for assuming the twinkle in her eye was attraction and interest. Well, the "on top" comment was kind of a neon sign of interest, and I thought about it often. The way she'd said it. The way it would feel to have her snuggled on top of me. Wiping my face, I tried to clear my head. It was way too soon for those thoughts.

Quietly, I walked back toward the kitchen and stopped to watch Layla. She hummed as she set plates and silverware on the table. Then she opened my junk drawer, picked up a pen and flipped the calendar pages and started writing. Later, I'd see what she added. While she was distracted, I tiptoed to her purse and dropped in a tiny frog. She hadn't said anything about the frogs yet, which surprised me. I'd tucked some into her apron when we were tangled on the floor. When I was at her house the next evening, I'd surreptitiously set one on top of her fridge, right near the edge. Yesterday, thanks to a little help from Lettie, a tiny purple frog made its way into Layla's car and onto the center console.

This giggly mermaid had captured my interest. I was far from a hermit. I'd dated, but mostly I'd gone out with women who weren't expecting a second date. But here I was, thirty years old, and seeing this short curvy woman in my kitchen had me envisioning a happily ever after, something I didn't even care about weeks ago. I was hiding frogs for her to find, hoping that she'd recognize it as my doing... hoping she'd take a chance on me and that I could be her prince.

"I can feel you looking at me." She spun around and propped her hands on her hips. "What?"

My gaze swept over her, landing on her feet. "Barefoot?"

"I wore shoes, but I kicked them off when I walked in." She dropped into a chair. "It's all ready."

Not only had she made me dinner, but she was barefoot in my kitchen. And I liked it. A lot.

I sat down next to her, and she gripped my hand. "Tell me something bad about you."

"Is this because you like bad boys and need convincing?" I thought through all the things I'd ever done that qualified as bad. Many of them I'd be happier if she never knew about.

She let go of my hand and served herself food, then nudged the bowl toward me. "No one is perfect."

The woman had to be a master at riddles. Her statements, seemingly unconnected had so far all led to a final point, which joined the threads. Or was she saying she wasn't perfect because she liked bad boys?

"How bad are we talking? Locking a squirrel in my brother's room because he asked out the girl I liked? Or..." I stabbed my fork into the bowl of mac and cheese. "Or being the guy who doesn't call a woman again after a first date?"

"Ever?" Her brown eyes were full of emotions, but there were so many, I couldn't sort them out.

Pretty sure disappointment was in there somewhere.

"Still want to go out with me?" Staring at my bowl, I kept my hand on the table but didn't move it closer to her. I wanted her to grip it again.

Her chair shifted backward, and she padded over to the wall calendar. Her finger moved from the day marked in red to the day after. The quiet was dragging on far too long.

I stood and walked up behind her. "Some of them were nice, I suppose, but none of them occupied my thoughts when I wasn't with them... other than feeling guilty about not calling."

She grabbed my hands and pulled them around her waist. "Is that why we're *talking?*"

"Part of the reason." I closed my eyes and rested my chin on top of her head, being more honest than I'd ever dared or cared to be before. "I spend more time thinking about you than I spend on any other single topic."

"What about married topics?" She giggled, sending high-voltage electricity dancing through me. Then she leaned back and dropped her voice to a whisper. "What's the other part?"

"When you didn't accept my invitation for a date—I'm glad you thought about it more—I decided I needed another way of getting to know you."

"Showing up to the doughnut shop on Tuesday was sort of like calling after a first date. After a really long first date that involved kissing."

I wished I could see her face. From the sound of her voice, I knew there was a wide smile tugging at her lips. "I guess it was."

"And I've seen you every day since." She tilted her head back. "Your poor brother. And that poor squirrel. What was her name?"

"I don't remember." I scooped her up and carried her back to the table. "I want to eat before I have to leave for work."

"I sort of like it when you go all caveman." She took a bite and wrinkled her nose. "It's cold. Let me warm it a bit."

I was going to exhaust every last shred of my willpower and restraint to make it another fifteen days without kissing her. Why had I said only talking? We could have been developing a talking *and* kissing habit.

CHAPTER 11

LAYLA

J dumped the contents of my purse onto the bed because carrying a small purse that could be worn cross-body would be better for tonight's date. I separated out old receipts and anything else I didn't need with me but stopped when I found a small plastic frog.

"Lettie, why must you tease me? Eventually I'll tell him about Prince Nicolaus."

She leaned around the doorframe. "What are you talking about?"

I held up the frog. "There were four of these in my apron at work. One in my car, and now I find one in my purse."

"Not my frogs, but I did see one on top of the fridge this morning. I thought you were trying to be funny." She shrugged. "Should we call an exterminator?"

I ran to the kitchen and snatched the pink frog off the top of the refrigerator. Four at the shop plus the one in my car and the one in my purse and the one on the fridge… seven frogs. "What day did I have that party? Sunday, right?" How could I not remember what day I'd met Nico?

"Don't know. I was out of town, remember?"

"You aren't being helpful. Yes, Sunday because Nico took me to breakfast on Monday, and the shop was closed. But then he came in on Tuesday." I counted days on my fingers. "There are seven frogs. Nico is counting the days."

"You already said he was marking days off on his calendar."

"He knows I like frogs, and he chose an odd number of days. He's giving me a frog for each day." Tomorrow, I'd bring those little frogs home with me from the shop. I lined up the three I had on my dresser. "Don't they look cute all lined up?"

"Y'all are weird."

"He's being sweet. There's got to be something you like." I sat on the edge of the bed. "What do you like?"

"Not what. Who? I like Archer."

"Maybe you should get him a frog."

She rolled her eyes. "Have fun tonight. I'll be asleep by the time you get home."

"I'll be quiet, and I promise to be in time for work."

"Good because I can't run that place by myself. I make the doughnuts. You sell them."

After another glance in the mirror, I pulled off my shirt and ducked back into my closet. I flipped through all my shirts, then put the original shirt back on.

It was so sweet of Nico to hide a frog for me each day. But how did he get one into my car?

"Lettie, did you help him with his frog project?"

She peeked around the door again, but now she had a toothbrush in her mouth. Her grin was answer enough.

"You're a sneak! And thank you." I walked toward her, intending to hug her.

Shaking her head and pointing at her toothbrush, she backed out of the room. Lettie wasn't really the touchy type. Even I could admit that hugging while brushing teeth was weird.

Staring at my purse stuff dumped on my bed, I made an impulsive decision. My credit card got slipped into my phone case, and the phone went into my boot. I wouldn't take a purse at all.

Standing right by the door, I yanked it open at the first sound of a knock. Nico looked just as amazing out of uniform as he looked in uniform.

He grinned as his gaze swept over me.

"Let me tell Lettie that I'm leaving."

Nico stepped inside and closed the door behind him. "You look amazing."

"Are you trying to make me blush?"

"Is it working?" He crossed his arms and leaned on the doorframe.

"As if you can't tell." Forcing myself to walk away from him, I hurried down the hall. "Lettie, he's here. I'm headed out."

"Have fun… talking." She wiggled her fingers. "I can't wait to hear about it tomorrow."

Before starting back toward the living room, I sucked in a deep breath. A tiny part of me was concerned about Nico's penchant for not calling women after the first date. Not only did I want tonight to be fun and memorable, but I also wanted to talk to him tomorrow and the next day.

When I returned to the living room, he was still leaning against the wall. "We should go if we're going to make our reservation time."

"Reservations?" In this area, reservations meant one place, a place with a chef I really didn't care to see tonight, but since Nico had gone to the effort of planning such a nice dinner, I was going to keep my mouth shut and hope we didn't bump into the Cowboy Chef.

"At the winery." He held out his hand.

I laced my fingers with his, then locked the door one handed. After staring at the keys a second, I glanced down at my boot. I hadn't planned for where to stash my keys, and I didn't have the option of not taking them with me.

"I'll put them in my pocket."

I dropped them into his hand. "Thanks. I guess that means I can't ditch you in the middle of the evening."

His eyebrows shot up. "Ditch me?"

I pressed up against his chest, inching up on my toes. "What would be the fun in doing that?"

A chuckle rumbled in his chest.

We strolled out to his truck, and he helped me in as always. Well, not exactly as always. He didn't pick me up and set me in the seat this time. And I didn't grab his shirt and kiss him before he walked away. As much as I wanted another kiss—because so far, every kiss had been better than the last—I was enjoying getting to know him.

The drive to the restaurant didn't take that long, and I was sorry it was such a short drive. Nico's thumb brushed over the back of my hand as he drove. Protective and kind, he made me want to skip ahead—way past the first date—and think about weddings and white picket fences.

When we were almost to the door of the restaurant, I tugged on his arm. "I need to tell you something."

"What's up?" Still holding my hand, he tucked our joined hands behind me and pulled me close. "Everything okay?"

"I'm fine, but in case it gets weird—I'm just going to tell you."

"But not before your halted and cryptic statements ramp up my curiosity." He gazed down at me. "What's got you so tense?"

"The very first week I moved here, I met this guy at the grocery store, and he invited me over."

Jealously flickered in Nico's eyes, but he nodded, silently prodding me to continue.

"Nothing happened. His friends were there. They were nice. And after I left, I never saw him again." This would've been a good time to mention that I was the woman who rarely got called back for a second date, but I didn't. "I didn't see him in a dating kind of way, but I see him around town."

His eyes narrowed as if he was thinking hard. "Your true confession somehow relates to this place?"

"I had lunch with the Cowboy Chef. His name is Jeffrey."

Nico's hand tightened around mine. "I know him."

"He was a gentleman, so it's not like he's a bad guy or anything. It's just awkward sometimes. He wasn't a fan of giggling." I watched Nico's chest rise and fall, wishing he would say something instead of just gazing at me.

"Do you want to stay?" He glanced at the door and then out toward his truck.

"I do. He's a good cook, just not dating material. For me, at least."

Nico's lips curled into a small smile as he pulled open the door. "Next time we go out, we'll choose a different place. Tonight, we'll just hope we don't bump into him."

"Next time?" My words came out much breathier than I'd intended, and there were probably stars dancing in my eyes.

His stubble tickled my cheek when he leaned close. "Yes, and hopefully many times after that."

CHAPTER 12

NICO

$\mathcal{A}$fter a fabulous dinner where we did not see the Cowboy Chef, Layla and I strolled into the dance hall. I'd been looking forward to this part of the evening since she'd agreed to go out with me. Not only did I love dancing, but knowing she'd be in my arms all evening was the cherry on top.

"What can I get you from the bar?" I helped her onto a tall stool at a bar-height table.

She chewed her bottom lip and tapped a fingernail on the table. "I think… since you are driving, I'll have a margarita."

"Coming right up." I brushed a hand down her back. "Then we'll dance."

The line at the bar was short, and after only a minute, the woman behind the counter asked what I wanted.

"I'll have a margarita and a bottle of water." I handed her cash when she set the drinks on the bar. "Thanks."

As I set Layla's drink on the table, someone patted my shoulder.

"Nico, fancy seeing you here." Dag grinned, then turned his attention to Layla. Pointing at the drink in front of her, he lifted his eyebrows. "You old enough for that?"

My cousin was six years older than I was, and if he was breathing, he was flirting. I debated whether I should let him talk himself into a corner or I should be kind and stop him.

Layla picked up her drink and took a sip, but then her gaze snapped from Dag to the woman standing beside him.

Goldie grinned and stuck her hand out. "I'm Goldie. Don't mind Hidalgo. He thinks he's funny."

"Usually when someone is funny, other people laugh." Layla shook Goldie's hand. "It's nice to meet you. I'm Layla."

Biting back a laugh, I tucked an arm around Layla. "She works at the doughnut shop. And unlike some people"—I patted Dag's shoulder—"she's funny."

Dag tipped his hat. "Forgive my attempt at humor. So you work with Tessa?"

"For about a month now. I really like her."

He nodded. "She's pretty great, at least if you listen to what Garrett says." He tugged an empty stool away from the table and motioned for Goldie to sit down.

"You know the Henrys?" Layla leaned against me and sipped her drink again.

Goldie laughed. "We both work out there. Hidalgo is a ranch hand, and I'm a housekeeper."

Dag nudged her. "She cooks too." He dropped onto another stool and used his longneck bottle to point at Layla. "I guess she's the reason you need me to go out with Brian's third wheel."

Layla set her drink down and slid off her stool. "I like this song."

"Excuse us." I grabbed her hand and led her out to the dance floor. "Listen, Dag isn't horrible, he just—"

She reached up and put a finger to my lips, then inched closer. "I feel awful for his girlfriend. I can't believe he's talking about dating other people when she's right there."

I spun her, giving me a second to refigure my thoughts. I was prepared to talk about Dag calling the woman a third wheel and how I wasn't going to go out with her again. But Layla never ceased to surprise me.

I leaned down to talk to her. This was when the height difference was a bit of an issue. "Dag and Goldie are friends. They've known each other since high school."

Her brow furrowed. "But it's completely obvious that she likes him."

"My cousin is a nice guy, despite his comments, but he can be obtuse." I'd gotten out of an awkward conversation pretty easily.

She patted my chest. "I can see that. Now, tell me about this third wheel you can't go out with again."

I gazed down at her. "My friend Brian, the guy who towed your car, asked me to go out with his girlfriend's cousin or friend. Something like that. We'd gone out once before when she was in town, but I told him I wasn't available and connected him with Dag."

"Oh." She leaned her head on my chest, and we danced without talking through another three songs.

Even after that we danced. When the music was fast, I spun her and dipped her, loving the sound of her laughter. When the music slowed, I held her close. It wasn't even a question that I'd call her again, but hands down, this was the best first date I'd ever had. It helped that we'd talked so much this week and weren't strangers. Her off-the-charts adorableness—if that was a word—figured into it a bit.

"Whew. I need a break." She pulled her hair off her neck.

I watched as it landed on her shoulders, cataloging the spots so that later, much later, I could drop kisses in every place her hair had touched.

She laced her fingers with mine, snapping me out of my daydream. "You are incredible on the dance floor. It's like your hand on my back tells my feet where to go. I've never had this much fun dancing."

"That makes two of us. You make a great dance partner."

As we walked back toward our table, she squeezed my hand. "Going out with that woman… was that why you had a favor you could call in?" Layla clearly didn't forget much.

"It was."

She stopped before we reached the table and clasped my other hand. "Don't say anything to Dag."

"About?"

She rolled her eyes. "He needs to figure out his relationship with Goldie, and telling him would make it way too easy."

"I won't say a word."

"Good, and I'm glad you didn't go out with that other woman again." She spun around and strolled back to the table.

I'd have to thank Dag later when I wasn't telling him that his beautiful friend liked him.

Hanging out with Layla was helping me see things I'd never bothered to notice before. As I walked to the table, I watched how she chatted with Goldie, open and engaging, like she'd been the day we met. Not even an allergic reaction had dulled her spark.

She giggled at something Goldie said as I walked up to the table. The sound was magical, and my grin probably reflected my thoughts.

Dag nudged me as I picked up my water. "Does that hook in your cheek hurt?"

"Feels better than I expected." That wasn't a lie. I normally avoided anything that even resembled commitment, but now I was scheduling my life around Layla's free time and hiding frogs for her to find. "Is it that obvious?"

Dag pressed a hand to his heart, then opened and closed his eyes, making a horrible attempt at fluttering his lashes.

Layla looped her arm around mine and leaned against me. "I've enjoyed every minute, but I need to be up early to serve doughnuts."

"Your carriage awaits." I smiled as she slid her hand down my arm and interlocked our fingers. "Night, y'all."

"My little cousin has a girlfriend." Dag laughed.

Goldie smiled as she swatted his arm. "Bye. It was nice to meet you, Layla."

After helping Layla into the truck and climbing into my seat, I pulled out of the lot. "I had fun. Maybe, if you want, we could go fishing one afternoon. Or whenever you're free."

"Will I have to put worms on the hook?"

"I can handle that."

"And if I catch something, could you take it off the hook?"

"Sure."

"Then, yes. I'd love to go fishing with you." She adjusted her seat belt as she turned to face me. "I love the frogs. Some are still at the shop because I hadn't figured it out yet and thought maybe a kid had dropped them. But I know right where they are, and I can't wait to have the collection all lined up on my dresser. And when I get home tonight, I'm going to hunt for the one you hid while I was talking to Lettie, so don't tell me where it is."

"I won't tell you." I kissed her fingers. "Since you like kissing frogs and are on the hunt for a charming prince, I thought I'd help that process along."

"Did you know that in the original fairy tale, the Grimm one, that she didn't kiss the frog?"

"I didn't. How did she get him to turn into a prince?"

"In the original, he asked to sleep in her bed, and she threw him against a wall."

"Can't really blame her for that."

"Right? Anyway, when he hit the wall, he changed into a prince."

I laughed. "Ouch. That really changes the whole story, doesn't it?"

"Just a bit." She giggled. "It's a shame too."

"Why is that?"

"I don't think I could throw you even an inch." Grinning, she turned and stared out the window.

Yep, I was hooked. And thanks to a little help from Lettie, my frog had jumped from where I'd left it on the mantel onto Layla's pillow. In light of my newfound fairy-tale knowledge, I highly anticipated her reaction.

CHAPTER 13

LAYLA

*W*earing my favorite frog jammies, I curled up in bed and stared at the little frog on my pillow. Lettie had to have helped Nico get it here because surely I would have noticed a man his size sneaking down the hall behind me, but it didn't matter. The biggest surprise was that he'd asked her to put it there before I'd told him about the original fairy tale.

I snapped a picture of the plastic toy sitting on my pillow and texted it to Nico.

He replied right away. *You didn't throw it against the wall?*

It's possible I may have already found my prince. That was the stupidest, most impulsive thing to say after a first date, but that didn't stop me from hitting send.

I stared at the phone, waiting for a reply. One minute stretched into two, then three. "Good job, Layla. You did it again." Rushing into things was my specialty. The stars in my eyes often blinded me to reality. Nico felt different, but apparently, he was just like other guys, scared off by the idea of forever.

With all the force I could muster, I flung the plastic frog against the wall. As it bounced on the ground, my phone rang.

"Nico?"

"I made it all the way to the truck, but if I drive over to see you right now, it will keep you up way too late. And I don't want to do that. So, I'm back inside, wishing I could snap my fingers and pop up next to you."

I wiped tears off my cheeks. "Hang on a sec." While I found the frog on the floor, I switched the call to video and was treated to a view of a shirtless Nico. "You aren't wearing a shirt."

He grinned. "I ran out the door in a hurry. It's probably best that I don't race across the county line right now." The phone jiggled a second, and then he reappeared, stretched out on his side with a hand propping up his head.

"I thought my comment scared you off."

"Not at all. You make me believe in fairy tales. Before, I thought they were only in the pages of books. Now I know better."

"Will I see you tomorrow?"

"I feel a craving for doughnuts coming on."

I giggled, then slapped a hand over my mouth, not wanting to wake Lettie. "I had a great time tonight."

"I did too." His hand neared the phone. "I should let you go."

"One last thing."

"What's that?"

"Thank you for not rushing things. I know we've talked every day—"

"And seen each other."

"Yes, but it's been nice. We've talked. It would be far too easy to get caught up in this current and get hurt." I stared at the little frog. "I've made that mistake before."

"Want me to tell you a bedtime story?" His grin promised entertainment.

"Yes, I absolutely do." I propped my phone up and snuggled into my pillow.

"Once upon a time, there was a beautiful mermaid. There was a great storm, and she found herself on dry land far away from the ocean."

My giggles only spurred him on.

"A prince, who thought he was only a frog, hopped to her rescue. He wasn't as strong as he hoped to be, but one kiss from the mermaid, and the frog started to change. The end."

"What about the rest of the story?"

"We're still writing it." He pulled the phone close to his face. "I'm loving every word of our tale."

"Our mermaid tale."

He chuckled, and I wished my head was against his chest to hear the chuckle rumble inside. "And a whopper of a tale it is."

* * *

NICO WALKED into the doughnut shop when the crowd was thin, which meant I could talk to him. He set a tiny frog on the counter before dropping onto a stool.

"How are things going, my beautiful mermaid?"

"Swimmingly!" I handed him a coffee mug. "And even better now."

He winked as he got up to get coffee.

After lining up the little frog with the others, I grabbed his favorite doughnut and set it in his spot. "Big plans today?"

"I need to make a run to the grocery store, then meal prep

for the week. And then, because of all these doughnuts I keep eating, I need to spend some time working out."

"Working out? That sounds like fun."

His eyebrows shot up. "You like to work out?"

"Don't sound so surprised. But not really. However, watching you work out would be great fun! That's what I was talking about."

A delicious smile spread across his face. "Just say when."

I helped a group of customers, conscious of Nico's gaze tracking me. While I was thoroughly enjoying talking to Nico every day and seeing him—we hadn't missed a day yet —my curiosity about how this would change after the twenty-one days was ramping up. And I had a feeling he was intentionally stirring that curiosity with the little bitty frogs.

When the wave of customers lulled, Nico slapped the counter. "I should go if I'm going to get anything done today. I could push my workout to this afternoon… until after the shop closes. You could come over."

"And I could make you dinner after an exhausting workout."

"Sounds perfect." He tapped the counter again. "See you later then."

"I'll see *you* later. Can't wait." I ran around the counter and stopped in front of him.

There were a few customers scattered around the room, but they didn't even seem to notice all the attention I'd been giving to Nico. Or maybe they noticed and didn't care. Either way, I didn't feel bad about chatting with him.

He smiled down at me. "Yes?"

"Want a hug?"

In the blink of an eye, I was off my feet and wrapped in his arms. With my face buried in the curve of his neck, I breathed in his cologne or maybe that was just bodywash. No matter what it was, it smelled like Nico.

"I like you." I kept my voice quiet, which ended up sounding all breathy.

He set me on my feet and brushed a knuckle down my cheek. "Same."

I'd say this day couldn't get any better, but that wasn't true. Later, I'd be watching Nico work out. My heart beat faster just anticipating the view of his muscles straining during exercise.

Actually seeing it would get my heart rate way up. That was the whole point of exercise, right?

EVEN THOUGH I had absolutely no intention of exercising, I changed into exercise leggings and a tank top before heading to Nico's. For late February, the weather was perfect. Days like this were the reason people put up with the heat in August.

I loaded grocery bags into the passenger seat, and then on the way to his house, I called my mom.

"Hi, Layla. How are you? You haven't gone over to your sister's house recently, and you haven't called. We were worried about you."

"I saw Issa just the other day. I'm fine. Better than fine, actually. I met this guy."

"Sweetheart, don't rush into anything. I don't want to see you hurt again."

Mom's vote of confidence was why I hadn't called. I reminded myself often enough of past failures. Having her bring them up had me wishing I'd kept my mouth shut.

"I have your recipe for Spanish rice written down, but I was hoping you could walk me through the steps."

"Now? It's a little early for dinner, isn't it?" That was Mom's way of asking for more information.

"I'm making dinner later for my friend. After we work out."

My mom had the audacity to laugh. Out loud. For almost a minute.

"I figured tacos for dinner would be good, and I wanted to make rice to go with it, but if you're busy, I'll just use the recipe."

"Darling, don't be mad. It's just—the thought of you working out is funny. You're beautiful, and I wouldn't change a thing about you, but I've never seen you even break a sweat."

Mom had no clue how warm those costumes could be. When I worked parties there was all kinds of sweat.

"I figured I'd try something new." Watching Nico work out was going to be something new, but now I was determined to break a sweat. It would probably only take a push-up or two to get me there.

"He must be quite the catch."

"He is. Listen, I'll be at his place soon, so I'll just—"

"Put the oil in the pan and sauté the bell pepper and onion a little before adding in the rice." She continued through the steps, refreshing my memory.

"Thanks, Mom."

"You're welcome. And, Layla, keep me posted. How long have you been seeing him?"

"A week and a half. We haven't made anything official or anything, but he's nice, and we see each other every day."

Mom stayed quiet.

"We talk and have dinner together. Last night, we went dancing. I like spending time with him."

"You sound very happy."

I turned into Nico's driveway and waved. "I am. Talk to you soon."

"Love you." Mom ended the call, and I jumped out, eager to try something new.

CHAPTER 14

NICO

$\mathcal{I}$ opened the garage and grinned as Layla pulled up the driveway. For someone who claimed they were only going to watch me work out, she sure came dressed for exercise.

Hips swaying, she strolled up to me with a grocery bag in each hand. "Let me put this stuff in the fridge; then we can get to the good stuff."

I took the bags and followed her inside. "I thought we were going to work out first?"

Her face scrunched up in that adorable way. "You are. That's the good stuff."

"Oh!" I chuckled, knowing full well what she'd meant the first time. "So you didn't mean dinner."

"I hope tacos are okay. I've never met anyone who didn't like tacos, so I thought that was a pretty safe choice."

"I like tacos."

"And I'll make rice. My mom taught me to make it just

like my grandma made it. I like to keep the chunks of onion and bell pepper big for people who'd rather eat around the veggies, but other than that, it's mostly like my grandma made it." She started unpacking bags as soon as I set them on the table.

Setting a hand on the table on each side of her, I caged her in. "You're making me your grandma's recipe? I feel special." I dropped a kiss on her shoulder.

She stilled, and for a half second, I wondered if I'd made a mistake. She'd thanked me for setting a slow pace, but there was nothing slow about this relationship… except that I was slow to kiss her again. She'd turned my thoughts inside out, and my life operated on a new schedule, one that revolved around seeing her.

After a deep breath, she turned and pressed her hands to my T-shirt. Desire swirled in her eyes, and when she licked her lips, I wasn't sure I'd make it the twenty-one days.

With her, I wanted things I'd never wanted before. Did I want to kiss her? Yes. But I'd wanted that before. Did I want more than that with her? Yes, but the same applied. I hadn't exactly been a choir boy. But the sight of her chatting about family recipes as she unloaded grocery bags had me envisioning domestic bliss. Before Layla, I didn't believe in domestic bliss. I'd figured the guys who raved about how in love they were had sipped some sort of tainted punch.

Her gaze swept over my face and landed on my lips. She swallowed, and it took every last ounce of determination not to taste her lips. Layla had said it best when she said that it would be too easy to get caught up and end up with someone getting hurt. She was the last person in the world I wanted to hurt.

"How did I get so lucky?" I brushed a loose strand of hair out of her face, then kissed her forehead. "Let me help you get stuff put away."

She gripped my T-shirt and smiled. "This will probably sound funny, but I'm going to say it anyway. I like you—you know that already—and I want you to kiss me. When the time is right. But every time you don't kiss me when it's obvious that you want to..." She tapped her chest. "Inside, I melt into a messy puddle of swoon."

"I'm glad that it's obvious what I want, and I can't say I've ever been accused of creating a messy puddle of swoon. Is there a merit badge for that?" I picked up the ground beef and other items that needed to be in the fridge and stepped away from her.

She rubbed my back. "You're a good guy, Nico."

For her, I wanted to be.

She looped her pinky around mine as we walked out to the garage. "You never asked why I was in a mermaid outfit."

I laughed, realizing she was right. "I guess I didn't. Why were you in a mermaid outfit?"

In the garage, she sat on the concrete floor and crossed her legs. "I'll tell you the story while you do your stuff."

Focused on stretching, I began my normal routine.

"I work at the doughnut shop, but until recently, I also had another job where I dressed up as characters for kids' parties and hospital visits. Stuff like that. It was fun, and seeing the kids brighten when their favorite character comes to life is just..." She pressed a hand over her heart and sighed.

"So you were a mermaid and made a little girl's birthday memorable." I dropped to the floor and started doing pushups.

Layla quieted.

"I'm listening." I glanced up.

She fanned herself, making a show of her admiration. "Uh-huh."

Having her around for workouts would be good. It guaranteed that I'd push myself.

"Anyway. I was booked for a job as a mermaid. It was kind of a mess though. The normal costume that I wear has a top that is like skin color—not exactly my skin color, but close—and has the bikini part just a different color. But that costume wasn't available, so I had to wear the other one with just the bikini top. And the space at the bottom for the feet is smaller. All of that was sorted out, but when I arrived at the party, I realized that nothing about that booking was good."

The change in her tone had irritation knotting my insides.

"It wasn't a kid's party. It was a bunch of college guys. Frat boys, I think. Needless to say, they didn't care about my balloon animals or my singalong."

Fueled by anger, I continued doing pushups long after I'd lost count.

"I didn't stay long. It was a good thing I didn't wear the bikini top that tied in the back. I made that mistake once, and some ten-year-old thought it would be funny to untie it. His mom didn't think it was funny. I bet he still hasn't gotten his Xbox back. That's why I was on that road. I left the party early and headed home. The next day, I quit that other job." She leaned close to me. "Um, shouldn't you like take a break or something. Consider me impressed. You don't have to do a thousand."

I pushed up off the floor and stood, anger still thumping in my chest.

"Whoa." She stepped in front of me and stared me down. "I've heard of red flames and blue flames, orange and yellow. But now I know what brown flames look like. I'm okay. Nobody hurt me."

"How do you expect me to react when I hear stuff like that?" I laced my fingers together and rested them on my head, feeling the burn from pushing myself and wishing my eyes didn't give so much away.

"I didn't tell you so that you'd run off on a rampage and hurt people. I'm just telling you about my life." She pinched her lips and inhaled. "Lots of people see me as weak and air-headed. I'm used to it, and I handle it."

"You aren't either of those things." I rested my hands on her waist. "Those people are wrong."

She avoided my gaze, her lips pursed. "If I wanted to be stronger, would you help me?"

"Do you want to start today? I'll help you get stronger and teach you self-defense moves that are more about balance and technique than strength."

"I'd like that. Because the part I didn't tell you was that there was one guy who helped me sneak out, and if it weren't for that guy—and for a lucky kick that probably left a toad singing soprano—that party might've ended differently."

I lifted her chin so that I could meet her gaze. "After what you'd just been through, I'm surprised you weren't..." I wasn't sure how to finish that statement.

I wasn't like those guys, and just the thought of her fear, which she'd tried hard to brush off, made my chest burn. But she didn't know that about me when I'd found her on the side of the road.

"Afraid of you? At first, I was too panicked because of the allergic reaction to think about that. I needed help, and you appeared. Kissing you was the first idea that popped in my head when I realized you needed a distraction." She crossed her arms. "Then I got a little caught up in being swept off my feet. Staying the night at your place was reckless. But, in my defense, the nurse did tell me you were a good guy."

"Really?"

"She also said you worked with her son, which confirmed that what you'd told me was true."

"But then when I asked you out—"

"I kissed you before I even knew your name. I didn't want

to go out with you if you thought… if that was the reason. The only reason."

I patted her hip. "Okay, we need to start with stretches. Those are important."

She caught my hand. "Before we start, I want to say one more thing."

"What's that?"

"Tessa stopped by the doughnut shop today after you left. She's back from her honeymoon and more in love than before she left. Anyway, you came up in conversation."

"When I said those things—"

Layla pressed a finger to my lips. "She said that you were probably a diamond in the rough and that Garrett said you were a good guy." Layla stepped away from me and put her hands on her hips. "Now, tell me what to do."

I'd obviously downed a gallon or more of that punch because I was thinking of how amazing it was going to be working out together every day. Would I tone down my normal routine so she didn't feel stretched beyond capability? Yes. Would I have to add an extra workout to my day to push myself when she wasn't around? Yes. Would I enjoy seeing her in leggings and a tank top? Absolutely.

CHAPTER 15

LAYLA

$\mathcal{I}$ stared at the pen on the ground, trying to decide if it was worth the pain of picking it up.

"What are you doing?" Lettie leaned out of the kitchen, her eyebrows raised.

Bracing my hands on my thighs, I squatted and choked back a groan. "Just picking up a pen. Don't mind me."

"Worth it?"

"No. I should've left the pen on the ground." I tossed it back beside the register. "I'm glad Tessa will be here today. That means I won't have to do as much walking."

Lettie laughed. "I meant the workouts. Are they worth the pain?"

"Totally, and I'm not saying that simply because Nico didn't wear a shirt the last two days. Today, we do more self-defense training. I'm way more excited about that than I should be."

She disappeared a second, then walked out, carrying a

tray of the pecan praline doughnuts. "I'm impressed that you are working out and doing the training. I can't even imagine trying to fight off a guy his size, any size. I eat tacos and doughnuts instead. Makes me harder to drag."

"Stop it." I hobbled over to the coffee pot to prep it for the morning rush. "Have you given anymore thought to talking to Archer?"

"Some. I decided that he's going to have to come find me. I'm here in town. If it's meant to be, our paths will cross."

"You moved all this way to settle for a maybe?" I walked closer to her.

She shook her head and backed away. "That's the best I've got right now. The upside is that I get to make doughnuts." Pointing at the door, she blinked away the threatening tears. "First customer is headed this way. You should unlock the door and tell Nico hello for me."

"He's here early!" I tried running to the door, and that lasted all of two steps.

When I flipped the lock, he pulled open the door. "You're hurting, huh?"

"Is it that obvious? I'm in horrible shape."

He glanced toward the kitchen, then leaned in close. "I happen to like your shape, darling."

"Flattery will get you a doughnut and coffee."

"Just coffee. I'm going to run home and sleep before it's time for our workout. I'm sorry the schedule is so tight today."

"You have to work. It's not a big deal. I'll bring dinner. Maybe I'll pick up barbecue."

"Only a few more nights on this schedule, then I swap back to days for a month. Dating will be easier then."

It was the first time he'd used that word. And while it seemed obvious that was what we were doing, hearing him say it out loud had me grinning like a toddler with a bag full of candy.

"We still on for going fishing day after tomorrow?"

"If you're still willing to do everything for me?"

He grinned as he filled his mug. "Then it's a date."

Tessa walked through the door and laughed as she propped her fists on her hips. "Nico, I hear you've been in here a lot."

"Go ahead. Poke fun. I picked up someone off the side of the road, and now I'm spending all my free time with her. I deserve all the jokes."

She twisted her hair up into a knot and secured it with a hair tie. "I'm not going to poke fun. Everything happens for a reason, and sometimes we're at the right place at the right time, and magic happens."

I filed those words away in my brain. I wasn't sure if this was luck, chance, fate, or magic. Did it matter? The result was Nico was now a part of my life.

* * *

I KNOCKED AS I pushed open the front door at Nico's. "It's me. I'll set the barbecue in the kitchen, then head into the garage."

"Meet you out there in a sec." Nico's voice was gruff, like he'd just woken up.

New mats lay on the floor of the garage. He'd cut his sleep time short to get these. I didn't want him cutting his sleep short, but I loved that he was thinking of me.

He yawned as he stepped into the garage. "Hey there." He hadn't even bothered to put a shirt on this time. No complaints from me.

"If you need to sleep more, I'll curl up on the couch and read for a bit. I don't mind."

"Nope. I'm good, and you're learning how to get free if someone pins you to the ground."

I didn't see any possible way for me to get a guy off me, but with Nico, I was willing to try. "I like the new mats."

"Since we'll be doing so much floor stuff, I figured a little more cushion would be good. Plus, if you flip me, I don't want to die."

"Right. Like that's ever going to happen."

He turned on the music, and I started stretching. We'd only worked out a few times, but I'd at least learned the stretches. Stretches were the easy part.

When we were all stretched and warmed up, Nico ran his fingers through his hair. "All right, get down on the mat. Flat on your back."

I lay down and nearly bit through my bottom lip when he straddled me and grabbed my wrists. I'd only have to lift up a few inches for my lips to meet his, but that was not the point of this exercise. At least today it wasn't.

"All right. If you end up like this, how would you get me off you? How would you get away?"

"Do you want me to try?"

"Yes. What would you do?"

"I thought you were going to teach me." I batted my eyelashes and was rewarded with a grin.

He leaned down so that we were nose to nose. "Imagine that I'm big and scary."

"But you aren't. You're Nico. And you would never hurt me."

Eyes narrowed, he scrunched up his face. "Imagine someone else. One of the frat boys."

I tried pulling my hands free and wiggling my hips. Nothing I did even moved Nico. After trying for more than a minute, I stilled, feeling rather helpless. "There's no way."

"There is a way. Look at how I'm positioned and picture

the legs of a table. If you want to knock over a table, you need to get it off-balance. Make sense?"

"Okay." I tried lifting my hips, thinking that might shove him forward. It didn't.

"Pull your elbows down toward your hips. You won't be able to push their hands up if someone has you pinned, but you will probably be able to move them along the ground. Try it."

After a deep inhale, I yank my elbows down, and surprisingly, they moved, pulling Nico's hands with them.

"So now I'm not as balanced. What is something else you could do to throw me off-balance even more?"

I lifted my hips, bucking him forward. While it felt like I'd toppled a giant, I was still under him, so clearly it wasn't exactly successful, except for the fact that my face was practically buried in his chest. That would be bad if it were anyone other than Nico.

"Good job. Now if you do those two things quickly, then you can use what I taught you about tucking the arm. And once my arm is tucked, buck me forward again and see what happens." He shoved his hands back to where they started. "Start from the beginning."

I yanked, bucked, tucked, and bucked. Nico landed to the right of my head, and I scrambled away as he rolled.

On my feet, I grinned. "I did it."

"You did." He grabbed my shoulders. "You're quick. Do you want to try it again?"

"Yeah. And don't go easy on me. I need to be able to do this." I stretched out on my back again.

He got into position again, and when he leaned down probably to whisper something sweet, I worked the routine, and freed myself.

Nico blinked from where he landed on the floor. "You caught me by surprise. Excellent tactic."

"What were you going to say?"

Rolling his neck from side to side, he stared at me. The tease dancing in his eyes made me giddy.

I stepped closer to him. "Sorry for saying you aren't big and scary. That's just because I know you. If I met you in a dark alley, then I might be scared."

"Might be?"

"You're kind of adorable, so I might be tempted to climb you like a tree."

He quirked an eyebrow. "We'll circle back to that later. Let's get started so I have time to eat."

"What were you going to say?"

"I'll teach you self-defense any day of the week." He kissed my forehead. "How's the muscle ache?"

"Better. I drank a lot of water. It helped, I guess."

"Good." He handed me weights, and we started our reps.

I'd completely lost my filter with Nico. Thankfully, he didn't seem to mind, and I was eagerly awaiting the last day of his just-talking habit.

CHAPTER 16

NICO

*A*ll the way to the river, Layla talked about who'd come into the shop today, how happy Tessa was now that she was married, and what she thought we should do for dinner. I loved when she shared her day with me. A day was just a tiny slice of her life. It was way too soon to think about sharing my life with her. For now, I was sticking to tiny slices, and maybe a few chunks.

I parked under a tree and helped her out before grabbing the rods, bucket, and tackle box. We were the only people on the bank that afternoon, which was perfectly fine with me.

Layla laid out the blanket and set the small cooler on one corner to keep the blanket from leaving us if a strong breeze came through. She eyed the tackle box as I readied the rods. "Are you using a lure or real worms?"

"Worms, but I won't make you touch them."

She stepped up beside me. "Thanks. I've never been fishing before."

That wasn't a surprise.

I baited Layla's hook, then wrapped my arms around her. "This is how you want to cast the line."

She leaned back into my chest. "Hmm? Do what? I'm distracted."

The more time we spent together, the more she flirted and the less she slapped her hand over her mouth to stifle her giggles. That made me feel like I was winning at this relationship stuff.

"You want me to just teach you how to fish all afternoon?"

Giggling, she tilted her head up to look at me. "Is that an option?"

"Most definitely an option."

Since meeting her, my ego had grown bigger, but so had my heart. I wasn't ready to make any rash declarations or hasty plans, but we hadn't even hit twenty-one days, and I was already thinking about the twenty-one months beyond that.

I showed her how to get her line into the water, noticing that any time her toes neared the edge, she backed up. "Layla, are you afraid of the water?"

She shook her head. "I'm a strong swimmer. If I had a pool, I'd spend all summer in it, near it, or thinking about it."

It was a bit too chilly to suggest we swim today, but I'd save that thought for later. I'd seen Layla in a mermaid outfit and had no doubt she'd look amazing in a swimsuit.

"What kind of fish do you catch here? Is the water deep?"

"Largemouth bass and catfish mostly. And right here, it's not too bad, maybe just above your waist." I let go of her and picked up my rod. "Keep it in the water, and if you feel a tug, pull on it a little. Just real quick."

We stood on the shore, waiting for the fish to bite and chatting about why I'd become a deputy, what she'd studied in school, and whether chili should have beans in it. It shouldn't. She didn't agree, but I forgave her.

When her rod moved, she yanked on it, and before I could drop my rod and wrap my arms around her, whatever she'd nabbed reacted and tugged Layla into the water.

"I'm so sorry." It surprised me that she'd caught anything, and it was even more of a shocker that she'd caught something big enough to pull her into the water. I waded in and held out my hand to help her up.

Instead of grabbing my hand, Layla wrapped her arms around my neck and shinnied up my body. She wasn't joking about climbing me like a tree.

But what I'd envisioned when she'd said that before differed from this reality in two ways: Layla's clothes were soaked with smelly river water and there was a fishing rod in her hand with a flopping catfish at the end of the line.

She seemed almost unaware that she was still holding the rod. The line swung around me, and I batted the fish away from her.

"Sweetheart, are you okay?"

With her face buried against my shoulder, her head moved back and forth, and her heart rate, which I could feel thumping on my chest, was elevated.

"What's wrong? Why are you clinging to me like a baby koala?" I held her tighter with one arm while trying to grab the fishing line with the other. "Did you get hurt?"

She pulled her legs up higher and wrapped them around me. "I'm not hurt."

"Are you cold? I have an extra sweatshirt in the car." I caught the line and held the fish out to the side so that it didn't accidentally touch her.

"I don't want to be in the water because of the fish." She turned her head to the side, and her eyes widened in fear. "A fish."

"You caught it. How you hung onto the rod baffles me, but you managed to fall in and still catch a fish."

She started her climb again and burrowed her face. "I'm terrified of fish."

When I chuckled, she swatted my chest and slipped ever-so-slightly lower. Then she clutched my neck tighter. I shifted her back up and kept her feet out of the water as best I could. "Afraid of fish? They won't hurt you. Not too badly. If you get poked with a spine, that hurts."

"I once watched a show where a bus crashed into the water, and fish ate the people. Ever since then, I've had nightmares about fish." The waver in her voice left no question about her terror, no matter how unreasonable.

"Piranhas aren't native to Texas. And I'm pretty sure catfish don't eat people." Who was I to judge unreasonable fears? I was the one who'd cut my head open because of a—this was a bad time to even think the word. I had a fish in one hand and my favorite girl in the other, who was terrified of the fish.

She sniffled. "I know that, but it doesn't make any difference to my brain. I know it sounds stupid."

"Hey. I don't think you're stupid." I took one step toward the shore and quickly discovered a small problem. "I need you to hang onto me really tight because I have to let go of you long enough to unwrap the fishing line from around my legs."

"Okay." She hung on so tight that I wasn't sure I'd be able to breathe deeply.

After unwrapping the line and taking the rod out of her hand, I dropped the fish into the bucket and the rod beside the tackle box. No longer distracted by the fish, I held her against me as I picked up the blanket and pulled it around her. "I am curious about why you agreed to come fishing with me."

"I wanted to spend time with you doing something you like to do." She used the corner of the blanket to wipe her face. "Sorry about messing everything up."

"You didn't mess anything up." I kissed the side of her head, ignoring the fact that she smelled like the river. "Let's get you home. Your place or mine?"

She giggled, as I hoped she would, since that question had been asked before. "We could pick up clothes from my apartment, then go to your house. Or is that too far out of the way?"

"Works for me." The only problem with my idea was that to go anywhere, I'd have to let her go. I didn't want to because holding her felt all kinds of right.

"You don't think I'm weird?" Her whispered question sent puffs of breath tickling my neck.

"I think you're weird in the most glorious sense of the word, and I wouldn't have it any other way." I kissed the side of her head again. "I think you should have asked that question when you had that mermaid costume on."

Her lips grazed my neck, and every nerve in my body danced a jig. "You're funny."

Maybe it wasn't too soon to admit a few things to myself. Was there a timeline for falling in love?

Layla wriggled down and threw off the blanket. "Look! Tiny frogs. Maybe I can catch one." She lunged toward a critter, then wiped her knees and tried again and again.

I crossed my arms and enjoyed the scene.

Fish scared her, which brought up all sorts of questions about her as a mermaid, but she loved frogs. She was simple and complicated, adventurous and hesitant, and smart and silly. I wasn't sure how so many layers could be inside that short, beautiful woman, and I was excited about all the layers yet to be discovered.

As she ran toward me with her hands closed, I pulled another plastic frog out of my pocket.

She opened her hand and showed off the tiny frog she'd caught. After only a second, it hopped off and disappeared into the grass.

I set the plastic frog in her hand. "Seems like a good time to give you this."

Biting her bottom lip, she stared at the frog a moment before meeting my gaze. "Only a few more until I collect all twenty-one. What happens then?"

"We'll just have to see."

A kiss. That was what would happen then, and I'd spent an inordinate amount of time thinking about it.

Waiting to kiss her wasn't about her at all, and I appreciated her patience. If I could spend this much time with a woman without kissing her and still wake up every morning with thoughts of her in my head, I knew this wasn't a flash of infatuation. My growing feelings for Layla were real. Very real.

CHAPTER 17

LAYLA

I waddled out of my bedroom with another outfit draped over my arm. "Okay, Lettie, be honest with me. I'm trying to decide what to wear tomorrow since it's day twenty-one. I can't tell you how many times I've counted those frogs today." I stopped in the living room. "Is the mermaid outfit too much or..."

"Yes. It's too much. You look like you're about to fall over, and you don't want doughnut glaze all over that costume. Weren't you supposed to give that back to the company?"

"I did. This one is new. Ordered it online." I held up the other outfit. "This one better?"

"That's adorable. He'll flip for the T-shirt with the frog wearing a crown, and those jeans fit you just right. I vote for that outfit. You just ordered that shirt, too, didn't you?"

"Yep. Do you think that he'll kiss me on day twenty-one or that day twenty-one is the last day of talking only?"

"I know what you're hoping."

"Is it that obvious? He doesn't care that I giggle. He likes me in spite of my irrational fear of fish, and he's so big and oomph." I pretended to squeeze an invisible Nico, which made Lettie shake her head. "I just mean he's tall, broad, and muscly. And I love it."

"It's obvious he's just as nuts for you as you are for him."

I couldn't help but grin because what she said was true. He made it obvious. If I was being played, he deserved some sort of acting award and a hard smack, and I didn't mean the kissing kind.

After waddling back to my bedroom and wriggling out of the tail, I pulled on my frog jammies.

Lettie called out, "You feel like cooking? Because I don't. I vote we pick up barbecue."

"Good idea. I hadn't even thought about dinner." I glanced at my phone. "Usually when he isn't working, I've talked to Nico at least four times by now, but so far today, I've only gotten a short text canceling our workout session. My muscles were happy, but my eyes were not."

"He'll call. Maybe something happened with work." She picked up her keys. "You going in your jammies?"

"Yeah." I pulled on a sweatshirt to cover the fact that I had on only a tank top. "You don't think something bad happened, do you? I've never heard of him getting called in on his day off. Would they do that? I like to think of him giving speeding tickets and writing up reports, but what if…" I stopped in the doorway.

She motioned me out, then locked the door. "No news is good news, Layla. If something was wrong, he'd have someone contact you."

Nodding, I followed her toward the parking lot. "You're right. He would do that… if he's alive." My phone vibrated, startling me. When I saw who was calling, I swiped to answer. "Nico! You aren't dead!"

"Not dead. Just dead tired." He almost didn't sound like himself because of heaviness, a weariness weighing down his words. "Sorry I didn't call earlier. Are you free right now? I thought we could grab a quick dinner."

"Yes. I can meet you. I just have to change out of my jammies. I know it's not even seven, but jammies are comfy."

"The frogs?" A hint of the usual Nico broke through with that question.

"The very same. But I can be ready in two minutes. Hang on a sec." I muted the phone. "Nico is coming to get me."

She waved. "Have fun. I'll see you in the morning."

"Bye." I clicked to talk again as I turned back toward the apartment. "Okay, I'm back. When will you be here?"

On his end of the line, there was movement, but he didn't say anything.

I stopped at the door and remembered that I'd left my keys because Lettie had hers. "Nico? You there?"

I felt his breath before I heard the words. "I'm right here."

Slapping a hand to my mouth to stifle my scream, I spun around and stared into his sad brown eyes. "What's wrong?"

"I'll tell you over dinner. Don't change. If you'd rather not go into a restaurant like that, I'll get it to go, and we can eat at my place."

"Sure. And that's good because Lettie has the keys."

He hooked a thumb over his shoulder. "She just went that way. We can probably catch her." He turned, then stopped. "Or you could stay at my place, and I could just have you back here in time to get ready for work. No funny stuff. It would be just like last time."

"I have to be up really early."

He caught my hand. "So do I, and I could use the company tonight."

I threw my arms around his neck. "I don't know what's wrong, but I hate seeing you so sad."

He lifted me off my feet, and I wrapped my legs around him.

When we arrived at his truck, he set me down. "What sounds good?"

I shrugged. "I'm happy with—"

"Don't say *anything*. I need you to decide. My brain isn't capable of that right now."

"I want sausage and mac and cheese. With a side of brisket, and if they still have any, a banana pudding."

He ran around and climbed in. "From the barbecue place?"

"I've stopped telling people how good they are because then it will be crowded all the time. Imagine if people in San Antonio figured out what a gem this place was."

He drove down the street and parked in the lot. "I'll be right back."

I watched as he hurried toward the building and ended up in line behind Lettie. What were they talking about? I'd have to grill her tomorrow at the shop.

Or sooner.

After glancing at my phone, I looked up and Nico was alone. And I stared. He was very nice to observe from afar or up close.

Rapping on the window nearly sent me flying through the windshield. Lettie grinned.

"Hey, I was—"

"Yeah, I know. You were watching your hunk. Is what he told me true?" There was a slight hint of accusation in her tone.

"I'm staying over there."

She rolled her eyes. "I meant about not having a key."

"Which is why I'm staying over there." I sort of thought those two things went together.

"Swing by and get your key on the way to his place.

Please. And I'm not worried about you staying over there because you only have twenty frogs." She jerked back as if I was going to swat her. I would've if I'd been a bit quicker.

"I only have nineteen because he hasn't given me one today. And I'll run up and grab them."

"Grab what?" Nico hopped in the truck.

"She needs her keys. I'm headed straight home." Lettie waved and rushed to her car.

I laid a hand on Nico's arm as I cradled the barbecue in my lap. "I'm still staying at your place."

"If you change your mind, I'll drive you home." He clasped my hand.

"I know. You're always a gentleman." That was one thing I loved about him, and that word wasn't used lightly.

I wasn't anywhere near ready to say it out loud, but the word crept into my thoughts more lately.

CHAPTER 18

NICO

Sitting on the floor near my coffee table, we ate in silence. Layla hadn't asked again what was bothering me, and I needed food before I could talk. Quiet and brooding wasn't normal for me, but she took it in stride.

"You can have the rest of the brisket. I'm stuffed, so I'm going to set the banana pudding in the fridge." She sprang up off the floor.

"Put mine in there too. I'll have it later." I ate a few more bites before carrying what was left into the kitchen. "I think I've had my fill too."

"I'll put it away. You go relax."

"I've been sitting most of the day." I leaned against the counter as she moved around the kitchen, putting food away and getting rid of trash. "I mentioned that I was going to help my dad this morning."

Her head bobbed up and down. "He was taking down a dead tree or something."

"Yeah. The tree is still up. We'd barely gotten started when Dad collapsed. Heart attack."

"Nico!" She slammed the fridge closed and wrapped her arms around me.

This is what I'd craved today and the main reason I'd called her tonight. Holding her close soothed something inside me.

Reluctantly, I released her. "He's alive. Overall, it looks hopeful, but there were some periods today where it was touch and go." I led her to the sofa and tugged her into my lap. "And as you can imagine, the whole thing was extra difficult because he was poked and prodded a lot."

Layla rubbed her hand on my shirt. "Did you pass out? You didn't get hurt, did you?"

"No, I just had to walk out of the room a lot, which meant leaving my mom because my brothers didn't arrive until later in the day."

"But she knows, right? I'm sure she doesn't blame you."

"She knows, and she wasn't upset. I just felt like I was letting her down. It's such a stupid thing to be afraid of."

Shaking her head, she poked me in the chest. "No, you have something that is fairly common. You wanna talk about a stupid thing to be afraid of? Fish."

I laughed in spite of my emotional exhaustion. "Can't argue with that."

"Hey!" She kissed my cheek, then shifted out of my lap. "Put your head in my lap. I'll run my fingers through your hair, but you might want to change first. You might fall asleep."

I couldn't think of a better way to relax. "Be right back." After quickly changing into sweatpants and a well-worn T-shirt, I strolled back out to the couch, trying to decide how to say all that was on my mind.

She patted the cushions. "I'm glad you called me."

"He has a procedure tomorrow. They are hoping to put in stents to help with the blockages, so I won't be around much. Again." I stretched out and rested my head in her lap. With my eyes closed, I savored the feel of her fingers trailing through my short hair. "I thought about you a lot today. One of the reasons was because the whole needle thing had me pondering Pavlov's dog. Think it's possible to train my brain to want a kiss from you every time I see a needle?"

"I am fully on board for helping with that experiment." She leaned down and kissed my forehead. "Just say when. Although you'll have to be careful when you get a flu shot after that training. You know, if I'm not there."

"Good point." I pulled her hand to my lips for a quick kiss, then let her go back to working her magic fingers. "Mostly I missed you just because. When they loaded my dad into the back of an ambulance, I wanted you there to tell me it was going to be okay. When I sat beside his bed, I wished you were there to hold my hand. When I left the hospital, I drove straight to your apartment."

Her fingers continued their therapeutic dance.

"I am way outside my—I can't even say comfort zone because with you, I'm perfectly comfortable—but I've never been in a relationship like this. I keep thinking you'll disappear like cotton candy left out in the rain or that you'll realize you can do so much better." I was too tired to filter my thoughts, and that last one earned me a swat. But it didn't make it any less true.

"Or maybe quirky you deserves quirky me. Do you want me to go to the hospital with you tomorrow? I can call Tessa and see if she'll cover things."

"As much as I'd love to have you there and for you to meet my family, I don't think Dad would want this to be the way you meet him. He wouldn't want you to see him like he is right now. So, for now, I'll say no, but if that changes, I'll call you."

"I'll keep my ringer on all day." She wiped her eyes.

"Aww, sweetheart, don't cry."

"These are happy tears, which makes me sound horrible because your dad is in the hospital, but I'm crying because you want me to meet them."

Somehow, no matter what was happening, Layla could make me laugh. "I'll allow happy tears. And I really do want you to meet them."

"I want you to meet my family too. We've known each other less than a month—which doesn't seem possible—but because I've talked to you every single day, I feel like I know you. The more I get to know you, the more I like you."

"Let's switch this up because I seriously might fall asleep, and with me like this, you don't have any room." I moved to the recliner end and leaned it all the way back. "You can curl up next to me like you did that night."

"What time do you have to be in San Antonio?" She pulled the blanket over her as she stretched out.

I tangled my fingers in her brown waves, which was equally as relaxing as having her fingers in my hair. "Sixish. I'll set an alarm for early, so I can take you home first."

"Okay. Wake me if you need anything."

"Oh! I almost forgot." I leapt out of the chair, rushed to my room, and dug the frog out of the pocket of my jeans. "Here."

She squeezed it into her fist. "Twenty."

"I'm really hoping I can see you tomorrow, but…"

Smiling, she settled back against me. "It's okay. We'll just see what happens."

That seemed like a good plan.

As I trailed my fingers through her dark hair, I closed my eyes. I'd for sure learned one thing these last twenty days. It didn't take twenty-one days to form a habit if it was something I really wanted.

Without a doubt, I wanted Layla.

CHAPTER 19

LAYLA

Sunday morning, I stared at the phone in the quiet shop while Lettie cleaned up the kitchen. I'd already talked to Nico twice today, and the after-church rush hadn't even started.

Garrett pushed open the door and let Tessa walk in first. "Good morning."

Tessa smiled up at him as she stepped inside. I'd never asked her how they'd met, but they acted like two people who'd known each other forever. Even the way he opened the door and she beamed at him as she entered seemed almost choreographed.

She kissed him before tying an apron around her waist. "I'll pack up a few doughnuts for you to take to the ranch."

"Sounds good." He leaned on the counter. "How are you, Layla?"

"Good. Besides the initial rush, it's been kind of quiet

around here." I checked my phone, wondering when I'd hear from Nico again.

"How many frogs do you have now?"

I snapped my gaze to Garrett's, which drew a laugh. "Oh, I guess Tessa mentioned the frogs."

Humor creased near his eyes. "She did. Nico's a good guy. Tell him I'm praying for his dad."

"I will." I'd grown up in a town that was small compared to a city, but not this small, and I was loving the connections in this place. And Nico didn't even live in this town, or in this county.

Garrett tapped the counter and watched Tessa as she walked toward him with a box in her hand. "I'm glad y'all met." He glanced at me, then back to Tessa. "You've probably heard the fable about the tortoise and the hare, and you've heard the moral of the story—slow and steady wins the race. But what we don't hear about is what happens after the tortoise crosses that finish line. Those guys know how to celebrate."

His grin made his point clear, and even if it hadn't, I wasn't going to ask him to explain. Clearly, Garrett knew Nico was being—slow wasn't the right word, but maybe measured—and was trying not to race into anything. I wasn't sure how Garrett knew, but he did, and now I was looking forward to the finish line, even if I had no idea how far away it was.

Tessa rested a hand on his chest. "Very true. You just never know what kind of interesting people you'll meet on the side of the road."

"In the dark." Garrett grinned, then gave her a peck on the cheek. "I'll be back at closing."

"Love you." She rubbed his shirt, then followed him to the door.

Once he'd walked out, I asked, "What was that about? You

acting all flirty with Garrett about me meeting Nico on the side of the road."

She laughed. "I wasn't talking about you. That's how—"

My phone rang, and I grabbed it. "It's Nico."

"Go talk. I'll cover the counter." Tessa shooed me toward the back door.

"Hey, Nico. How are things going?"

"He made it through just fine. They were able to address all the blockages." He sighed. "Mom is having a harder time today, so I'm going to stay here in town tonight." His voice wavered. "I'm sorry I won't get to see you. There's only been like three days we haven't seen each other, and I hate that today will add to that."

I swallowed, trying to keep the emotion out of my voice. "We saw each other this morning. It was still dark, but it counts. And I understand that your mom needs you."

Seeing the way he cared for his mom made Nico a hundred times more amazing in my eyes.

"I'll be back at the house tomorrow by ten if you still want to work out."

As much as I wanted to speed into town and hug him until the sun went down, I knew he needed space to be with his family, and I could give him that. "Sounds good. I'll be there."

"Sorry to keep bothering you at work today."

"It's fine. Tessa is working the counter. I let her know what was going on." I crossed my arms and pulled in a deep breath. "I'm glad you're keeping me updated and that I've gotten to talk to you."

Voices sounded in the background.

"I need to go, but I'll call again." A silence lingered. "And, Layla, just so you know, I've learned something since meeting you."

"What's that?"

"It takes far fewer than twenty-one days to form a habit that puts a smile on my face. And talking to you puts a smile on my face."

Big emotions threatened to rip open my heart. "You're just trying to make me cry."

"Now I've gone and done it." He chuckled. "Talk to you soon."

"Bye." The call ended, and I clutched the phone to my chest.

In twenty-one days, I'd forgotten about my attempts to stop giggling and curb my impulsive decisions. My giggling was back to normal levels, but my impulsiveness had declined. It wasn't because I questioned every decision and made the boring choice, but inside, I was more measured. When did I start using words like measured?

I wasn't chasing excitement anymore. I was too busy enjoying life.

* * *

Lettie handed me a banana pudding and a spoon. "You okay?"

"I am. It's just…" I shoveled a bite into my mouth. "It's day twenty-one, and I didn't get my frog. That's a stupid thing to think about. I know that, but that's what has me mopey tonight."

"You sure about that?"

"About why I'm mopey? Pretty sure."

She pointed down the hall with her spoon. "Go count your frogs."

The clink of my spoon hitting the table echoed as I ran into my bedroom. At the end of the line of frogs was a single Hershey's kiss. Running my finger along the line of frogs, I counted. One, two, three… eighteen, nineteen, twenty, twenty-one.

"You played the elf again, didn't you?"

Lettie leaned on the doorframe. "He slipped it to me last night at the barbecue place. I didn't even eat the chocolate. See what a good friend I am."

I hugged her. "The absolute best."

"He wasn't sure what would happen today, and he wanted you to end the day with a complete set."

"And a kiss."

"Yeah, but I'm pretty sure when he's thinking of kisses, he has something entirely different in mind."

"That makes two of us." I snapped a picture of the last frog and the kiss and sent it off to Nico with a text: *Can't wait to see you tomorrow.*

I'm looking forward to it more than you know. His response sparked tears and a smile. Dang the man's talent.

* * *

Two minutes before ten, I parked next to Nico's truck in front of his open garage.

Wearing only athletic shorts—and I presume something underneath them—he laced his fingers together on top of his head. "Hey there, you ready to sweat?"

He hadn't scooped me into his arms and kissed me until my toes curled, which had huge question marks dancing in my head.

I fanned myself as I drank in his beautiful display of muscles. "I think I'm sweating already."

When I stepped within reach, he tugged me to his chest, with one hand on the back of my head and the other on my back, he held me longer than he'd ever held me before. That wasn't insignificant because for a man determined not to kiss me until after the twenty-one days, he'd sometimes hugged me for several minutes as if that would somehow sate his other craving.

Maybe that worked for him. It didn't for me. I always left thinking about how it would feel to have his whiskers prickling my lips, his breath mingling with mine. All morning I'd been anticipating his kiss.

"Okay." He pulled away and clapped his hands. "Do we want to start with the routine or drilling some of the self-defense moves? I figured afterward we could go grab food somewhere."

I studied his face a second, trying to make the puzzle pieces fit. I knew the man wanted to kiss me. But he wasn't kissing me even though we were the only two people at his house, and there was nothing in the way of interruption. Why?

His house.

That was it. I'd said that very first night that there was going to be no kissing at his place. My feelings then differed from my feelings now. I was no longer simply infatuated, and I trusted Nico.

"Self-defense." I dropped my purse onto the bench and lay down on the mat. "Let's start with something fun." By something fun, I meant kissing, and within a few minutes, he'd know that too.

He straddled me and pinned me to the floor. Smiling, his gaze dropped to my lips a half second before he sucked in a breath. "Okay. Do you remember what to do?"

"I know exactly what to do." Instead of pulling my elbows closer to my hips, I lifted up and sealed my lips to his.

With a moan, he let go of my wrists, slid his arms underneath me, and cocooned me while he made up for all the days he'd been thinking about kissing me. His mouth moved against mine, his strong body pressing me to the mat.

He broke away, his breathing ragged and sexy. "I missed you yesterday." He rolled onto his back, keeping me wrapped in his arms. "Not because of counting days or even because of this. I just missed *you*. The sound of your voice is only a tolerable substitute for the feel of your hand in mine." He pushed my hair out of my face. "And the only reason I didn't greet you with a kiss was because you'd been clear about not kissing here."

"I know you better, and I know me better. I'm not ready for more than this, and maybe next time, we could do this someplace other than the garage floor, but that one little piece of chocolate wasn't nearly enough." I dotted kisses on his jaw. "And I do like being on top."

Chuckling, he pulled me down to him and tangled his fingers in my hair. His lips brushed mine, softly and gently, teasing a deeper and hungrier kiss. "The next habit will take longer to perfect."

"Oh? What's that?"

"I think—if you like the idea—I'll spend the next five months working on being the perfect boyfriend." He nuzzled my neck. "I mean, I've already been practicing, but practice makes perfect."

I nodded, loving the label, one that seemed obvious but hadn't been said. The timeline made my heart flutter a little. "I like the sound of that. A lot." I slid my arms around his neck and pulled him to me, finally getting that hungrier kiss.

By definition, kissing him wasn't impulsive because I'd been thinking about it since we'd walked into his house that very first time.

"When this kiss is finished, we'll go into the house." He touched his lips to mine softly between sentences. "With the whole odd number thing, is it tallied by day or in total? I want to make sure I get this right."

Laughing against his lips, I ran my hands down his chest. "In total, and I hope that soon, I'll lose count."

A chuckle rumbled in his chest, and I felt every bit of the vibration.

"Losing count. I like that goal. I can definitely help with that."

We didn't end up working out, at least in the traditional sense, but my heart rate was elevated for an extended period of time. That should count for something.

CHAPTER 20

NICO

Five months flew by faster than a barn swallow in flight. The old adage about time and fun was true. Dating Layla had upended my life in the best of ways.

I parked outside Layla's apartment, nervous and excited. Deep breaths helped calm me, but the sight of Layla in her tight-fitting jeans and her ruffly top sent my heart rate skyrocketing again. If I wanted to make it through the first part of our date without slipping up and letting on about the surprise party, I needed to calm down.

Standing on the sidewalk, she waved. And her grin was nothing short of spectacular.

"Happy birthday, beautiful. I didn't expect you to be waiting outside."

"I'm a wee bit excited." She held her index finger close to her thumb. "Just a little." As I stepped onto the sidewalk, she dropped her purse and launched toward me.

Of all the things I loved about Layla, the sheer delight

she exuded when I showed up ranked very near the top of the list. There was no question she loved me. We hadn't used that word yet, either of us, but I felt that way. And her love was evident in a million little ways and in a few big ways.

I caught her, wrapping her in my arms. Her legs circled my waist, and I greeted her like I hadn't seen her in days. Because I hadn't.

"Five days is too long." She rested her forehead against mine. "I missed you. Did you get everything finished at your parents' house?"

"Missed you too." Holding her against me, I picked up her purse and carried her to the truck. "We did. I'm not sure who had the idea to build a new deck in July, but we finished. Between that and work—"

"I know." She kissed me before shifting to her seat. "And I'm not upset. How are your parents?"

"Everyone is good. Looking at Dad, you'd never know he had a heart attack, but we didn't let him help too much. Mom kept asking when I was going to bring you to dinner again. We'll have to do that soon."

"I'd love that." She pulled me in for another quick kiss. "What are we going to do today? You've been quiet about the details."

I dropped her purse near her feet, then ran around and climbed in. Seeing anticipation and delight on her face only amped my excitement. "What do you think about butterflies?"

"Love them."

"I figured we'd start with a butterfly exhibit, have a romantic dinner, then go back to my place for dessert."

She danced her eyebrows and reached for my hand. "Dessert, huh?"

"Yeah." Brushing the back of her hand against my lips, I

glanced across the cab. "So, how did I do? Today is the last day of the five months."

"On a scale of one to ten, I'd give you an eleven." She giggled. "I still can't believe this."

"Believe what?" I turned onto the county road, headed toward the butterfly house.

"Us. This. It's just—" She shifted in her seat, slapping at her legs. "Pull over. Hurry."

I yanked the wheel and skidded to a stop in the grass. "What's wrong?"

Without answering, she launched out of the truck, kicked off her sandals, and started yanking her jeans off.

Struggling to not let her hot pink lace distract me, I ran up beside her, trying to understand why she was stripping out of her clothes on the side of the road.

A truck drove by, and I shifted my body to block the view of her. "Why are you—"

"Ants!" She swiped at her legs.

Then I noticed the ants on her legs and started brushing the tiny beasts off her thighs with one hand while holding her upright with the other.

"Did you get bit?" I picked her up and set her on the seat so that I could get the jeans off her ankles. Then I swiped more ants off her legs, trying not to notice what had been hidden under her jeans. They were pink. I'd already noticed that.

The panic in her eyes answered my question.

I reached for her purse, but it wasn't on the floorboard. "Layla, where's your purse?"

Her breathing was starting to change, and she grabbed my hand. "You put it by my feet."

I knew that. The Pixie Stix on the floorboard confirmed that. I glanced at the grass. The contents of her purse were strewn on the ground beside the truck. I picked up the epinephrine injector and gave myself a pep talk. "You can do this. Don't pass out."

Layla gripped my shirt. "I'll handle it. Just hold my hand and look out that way."

I pulled out the end, then handed over the needle. "I can do that. Count out loud for me."

With her forehead resting on my shoulder, she counted to eleven, squeezing my hand tighter than anyone would expect from someone her size. Five months of working out had made her stronger.

"I'm done with it. Will you put it somewhere? Just don't look at it." Her breath still sounded heavy.

Ants hadn't bothered her since the day we'd met. Why now? While they deserved partial credit for us meeting, today they were ruining the birthday plans.

"Let me pick up your stuff. Then we'll get you checked out. Do you have any Benadryl with you?"

She nodded.

I scanned the ground until I found her pill box and shoved everything else that looked like hers back into her purse. Ants crawled on the outside of her bag and completely covered one of her Pixie Stix. I left that one on the side of the road. The ants probably hitched a ride when she dropped her purse onto the sidewalk.

After shaking her purse and making sure there were no stowaways, I handed her two pills. "Let me grab water. I have a few bottles in the back seat."

She swallowed down the pills but stayed quiet, and that worried me.

"Layla." I leaned down to look her in the eye. "Are you okay?"

Her chest rose with effort. "It's not working. Usually, it works. But it still feels like someone is sitting on me." Tears brimmed in her eyes, ripping my heart into shreds.

"Do you have another injector?"

"I usually carry two." She pressed a fist to the center of her chest. "In my purse."

Instead of digging through her purse, I dumped it into the back seat. I didn't remember picking up a second injector, but maybe it hadn't fallen out. No such luck. There was no other injector.

"I can't find the other one." My brain raced. "Let's just get you to the hospital or the fire station. I bet the EMTs will have what you need."

"Nico." She grabbed my shirt. "If…" Sucking in a shallow breath after the word, she stared at me. "I don't make it…"

"Don't talk that way. You're just feeling panic because of everything." I whipped around and scanned the ground. Had I missed it in the grass?

Hearing the panic and desperation in her voice made my chest ache. I didn't want her thinking about dying, and I definitely didn't want to think about that.

She grasped the hem of my T-shirt. "Please."

Giving up my hunt, I faced her, not at all prepared to handle the tears sliding down her cheeks.

I clasped both of her hands between mine. "Tell me." If she needed to say something, I could be strong enough to listen. But I'd only give her about five seconds because then I was speeding to the nearest fire station.

"I love you." She blinked, then shifted as she leaned in for a kiss, more of a quick peck.

This was not how this story ended.

Not if I had anything to do with it.

I grabbed her jeans off the ground. "Hold that thought and hang on." I swung her door closed, and there on the ground was her other injector, tucked against the tire.

Now she wasn't the only one crying. But mine were happy tears.

125

In half a second, I had the end off the injector and the door open. "Incoming." That was probably a horrible warning, but that was the best I could manage.

When I jabbed it into her leg, she yelped in surprise. My thoughts boarded the needle train, and I blinked, trying to clear my head.

She touched my cheek, and my gaze snapped to hers.

Staring at her, my thoughts shifted to her admission and the panic swirling in my gut at the idea of losing her. "I love you too." This time, I was the one who yanked her to my lips.

Her squeak of delight made time slow.

I cupped her cheek, kissing her and completely forgetting to count. "I have no idea how long this has been in your leg."

"You love me."

It had to have been long enough. Without looking at the sharp end, I tucked this one with the other. "With all my heart. Now, let's get you checked out."

"I need pants!"

"It's easier to check you out without them." I winked.

Her giggle was a sweet sound because it meant she was breathing better. "Seriously. Let me just put them on. Did you check them for ants?" She scratched at her arms.

Hopefully the hives would start going down as the Benadryl worked through her system. I shook out her jeans and checked for ants inside and out before handing them to her.

"I'll turn around. Holler if you need help."

As soon as my back was to her, she pressed a kiss to the back of my neck. "I must've looked like a crazy woman yanking off my jeans on the side of the road."

"If I hadn't been so panicked, it might've been funny." I crossed my arms and willed my heart rate to slow.

"Pants are on. I'm sorry about ruining the plans."

"Ants ruined the plans. Not you. Besides, the L word was

a nice surprise." I made sure she was tucked inside before slamming the door.

Today was turning out nothing like I'd planned except for one part. While the doctor was making sure she was okay, I'd message Dag and Garrett and warn them about what was happening. My party plans were on standby, but I wasn't ready to give up on the surprise just yet.

CHAPTER 21

LAYLA

I blinked as we walked out of the brightly lit emergency room into the darkness. Unlike the last time I'd come here, this visit took hours. All the plans he'd made were shot.

"Nico, I'm so sorry."

His fingers were laced with mine, and he squeezed my hand. "I'm just glad you're okay and that you found out about the allergy stuff. Maybe that will help you."

I'd definitely be following up on allergy shots, and I wouldn't be taking Nico to those appointments.

"I ruined all your plans." My stomach rumbled from hunger, but I didn't feel like sitting in a restaurant. The hives were better but not gone, and being stared at by strangers wasn't how I wanted to spend the rest of my birthday.

"We're together. That's the important part. Why don't we head back to my place? Then we can figure out dinner."

I waited until he opened my door, then slid into my seat. "Yeah."

He'd spent a lot of time on his phone while the doctor and nurses fussed over me, so he must've been canceling reservations. Why was it that the end of the habits always seemed to go sideways?

I'd been eager for the end of the five months. It felt like a fork in the road, a possible change in direction.

We were both quiet on the way to his house, but his thumb brushed back and forth across the side of my hand all the way.

"You didn't pass out."

"I was more worried about you than the pointy thing." He shot me a side glance. "Then when you started talking about not making it…" His lips pinched, and he stared at the road.

"I was scared, and I wanted you to know how I felt." I leaned my head back and closed my eyes, appreciating how amazing it felt to have this big, strong man holding my hand. With him, I felt protected and loved. "It isn't that things are always perfect, but…" Lips pinched, I choked back the emotion that threatened to overwhelm me. "But what we have is good."

"I love you too, Layla. So much."

Nothing about his words surprised me, but hearing them out loud warmed me from head to toe.

"Please do me a favor." His voice was rough and sounded more like a plea than a simple request.

"What?" I tilted my head to look at him.

He pulled into his driveway, then pulled my fingers to his lips. "Stop carrying candy in your purse. Please."

"This was the only time—"

His brown eyes darkened. "I can't always keep you safe, but that won't stop me from trying. Please."

"Okay." I unbuckled my seat belt and hugged him as soon as he opened my door.

After an extra-long hug and a few kisses, he helped me out. "And I'd say what we have is better than good. How are you feeling? Any better?"

"I feel mostly fine. Just a bit jittery and a little sleepy, which is a strange combination."

"Let's get some food in you."

"And dessert." I bumped his shoulder.

The look he gave me made my toes go numb, and walking was more difficult with numb toes. Luckily, when I stumbled, his arm was around my waist in half a second.

"Careful, sweetheart, I don't want to have to take you back to the hospital tonight. I have other plans."

Now I couldn't even feel my feet.

He swung open the front door and waited for me to step inside.

I dropped my purse and kicked off my sandals. "What do you want to—"

The lights came on as a small crowd shouted, "Surprise!"

"Happy birthday, Layla." Nico's voice came out gravelly and yummy sounding.

I spun to hug him but gasped when I saw him.

Nico was on one knee, and he held a small velvet box. "Layla Tucker, I had a whole afternoon and evening planned, but this was the moment I was looking forward to the most. Months ago when I pulled over to rescue a mermaid on the side of the road, I had no idea that stopping would flip my world upside down and turn everything into sunshine and rainbows. I love talking to you, working out with you, and having you wrapped in my arms. Mostly, I love spending time with you. Will you spend all your tomorrows with me? Will you marry me?" His hand shook as he moved the box toward me.

"Oh, Nico. Yes." I slipped my arms around his neck and buried my face in his shoulder.

Cheers filled the room.

He stood, lifting me off my feet. "I love you, Layla. Your giggles. Your spontaneity. I love all of it."

"I need to tell you something, and it's okay for you to laugh."

He pulled back far enough to look me in the eye but didn't put me down. "What?"

"My frog—did you get him? He didn't get left in the grass, did he? I can't lose him."

"I made sure your frog prince made it into your purse."

Ignoring our audience, I brushed my lips on Nico's neck. "Good. I thought I was going to have to launch a search."

"Is that what you were going to tell me?"

"No." I dropped my voice to the softest whisper I could manage so that no one else could hear. "My frog's name is Prince Nicolaus. He was named long before I met you."

He grinned. "Just more evidence that we're living a fairy tale. Mind if I put you down and slide this ring on your finger? The way things are going, forest animals might start singing."

"Okay, but first…" I cradled his face and kissed him. "I'll always want one more kiss."

I never would've believed that kissing a tall, handsome stranger would be how I found my happily ever after, but then it happened.

Nico slipped the ring on my finger. "Happy birthday, Layla."

This was, hands down, the best birthday ever.

CHAPTER 22

NICO

*G*arrett helped Tessa into his truck, and when he leaned in to kiss her, I closed the front door. I had my own kissing to do.

"How are you feeling? Did you get enough mac and cheese?"

"I'm so full. And that cake was incredible. I'm not sure Tessa is real." Layla snuggled into the corner of the sofa.

"Be right back." I slipped into my room and slid her present out from under my bed. "Here. Open this."

She tore away the paper, then lifted the lid off the box. "It's beautiful." The box fell as Layla picked up the charm bracelet.

"I'm not putting a time limit on my next habit. But I want to add charms to this bracelet, marking our special moments. I started you off with a mermaid and a frog."

"This is amazing." She snuggled closer to me. "Even with the unexpected trip to the hospital, today has been pretty great. I need to call my parents. Have you thought about when you want to get married?"

I loved that she was already thinking about wedding dates. "You do need to call your parents. I talked to your dad a few weeks ago—over the phone—and he gave me his blessing. They knew this was coming."

"I'm surprised no one spilled the beans."

"As far as wedding dates, I'd like to hear your thoughts on the subject."

She blinked and chewed her bottom lip. Seeing her do that always made me want to kiss her.

"I don't want anything big, so planning won't take months and months. What about September? The weather then is usually nice. We could even have an outdoor wedding."

"We'd have to scour the grounds for ants."

She swatted my arm. "I'm being serious."

"Me too. I don't want anything to happen to you, and I don't want to pass out in front of all our guests when I have to jab your leg." I traced the soft curve of her cheek. "But September sounds perfect."

After wrapping her arms around my neck, she shifted into my lap. "Thank you for the surprise party. And for not changing those plans after what happened."

"I had everyone on alert, but once you seemed to be feeling better, I kept that plan in place. I've had the ring for a while, and I really wanted to hear you say yes."

"Will we live here?"

"If you want. With my job, I need to live in this county, so I can't pick up and move to Stadtburg unless I change jobs."

She brushed her lips on my ear, then feathered her way down my neck. "I like it here."

"Glad to hear that." September couldn't get here fast enough. "Are you thinking early September?"

She giggled. "Or late August."

* * *

TIME DID ITS MAGICAL THING, and here I was standing at the front of the chapel, holding my breath and waiting for Layla to walk through the double doors at the back of the room.

When the doors opened, I managed one quick gasp of air. Her strapless dress hugged her shape, then spread out in an explosion of ruffles. She looked very much like a mermaid without scales.

I adjusted my collar, and Dag slapped my shoulder.

"Don't pass out." He chuckled behind me.

She held my gaze as she marched up the aisle.

When her dad put her hand in mine, I croaked out, "Wow."

Grinning, she pulled that bottom lip between her teeth. If she kept that up, there was no way I'd make it to the end before kissing her.

As I looped her arm around mine, I leaned close. "You look amazing, and I can't wait to kiss you."

Her eyes shone with unshed tears as she nodded. "But first, we have to say our I-dos."

I was more than ready to promise Layla forever. Before meeting her, I didn't think fairy tales were real. Now I knew better.

EPILOGUE

LAYLA

I zipped up the side of my costume and adjusted my red bikini top. "When do I get to see your costume? I'm dying to know what you're going as to the Halloween party."

"You'll see." He'd closed himself into the extra bedroom a half hour ago. "I think you'll love it."

"Does it coordinate with mine? Isn't there a couple's prize?"

"There is, and with what I'm wearing, we might win."

My mind raced to imagine what costume coordinated with a mermaid. "Are you a merman? Are you going shirtless?" I dropped onto the bed, fanning myself. No matter how often I saw my hunk without a shirt, I was always impressed.

He poked his head in the door but not far enough that I could see what he was wearing. "I'm not going shirtless or as a merman. And you look amazing."

I slipped on my flats. "Let me move my things into my lobster purse, and then we can go."

"I'll be in the living room." He blew me a kiss.

After making sure everything I needed was stuffed into the lobster, I waddled out to the living room.

Nico stood in the middle of the room, wearing a smirk and a fisherman's outfit, complete with a net, a rod, and lures pinned to his hat. "Some guys catch fish, but I caught you. Great costume, huh?"

"Are you going to carry me around all night telling the story of how you reeled me in?"

"You bet your fins, I am. It's a whopper of a tale." He dropped his rod and net, then scooped me up. "What do you think?"

"It's perfect."

It didn't matter if we came home with the prize because, as far as I was concerned, Nico was my prize. He was everything I'd ever wanted and about four inches taller.

I loved my wall of a man.

* * *

WHAT TO READ MORE about the Cowboy Chef? Grab a copy of *Inspired by Mindy*.

When Jeffrey meets Mindy, he's instantly attracted. She's not his usual type, but he can't stop thinking about her. But there's no chance of romance because (1) she's younger than his new rules allow, and (2) she can't stand him.

Working with her isn't a problem. But being stranded with her definitely might be.

Also, Dag finds his happily-ever-after in the Cowboys of Stargazer Springs series. So does Lettie.

A NOTE TO READERS

Thank you for reading! When Nico first showed up at the hospital in Tessa's book, my critique partner asked if he was going to get his own story. I hadn't planned on it. But then she said she didn't really like him, so then I decided to write his story.

Layla first showed up on the page as a minor character in Helped by Ava, and I decided she needed her own story.

There is a little bit of fairy tale in almost every love story, and I wrote this novella with that in mind. I hope you enjoyed it!

Dag and Lettie will each get a story in the new series - **Cowboys of Stargazer Springs**.

Be sure to check out my website at www.PhreyPress.com for information about upcoming releases and to find other sweet romances and romcoms.

ALSO BY REMI CARRINGTON

Never Say Never

Three Things I'd Never Do
One Guy I'd Never Date
Two Words I'd Never Say Again
One Choice I'd Never Make
Three Rules I'd Never Break
Two Risks I'd Never Take Again
One Whopper of a Love Story
Christmas Love
Christmas Sparkle
Christmas Surprise

Stargazer Springs Ranch
Fall in love with cowboys and spunky women.

Cowboys of Stargazer Springs
The ranch hands are falling in love.

Bluebonnets & Billionaires series
Lots of money & even more swoon.

Pamela Humphrey, who writes as Remi Carrington, also releases books under her own name. Visit PhreyPress.com for more information about her books.

ABOUT THE AUTHOR

Remi Carrington is a figment of Pamela Humphrey's imagination. She loves romance & chocolate, enjoys disappearing into a delicious book, and considers people-watching a sport. She was born in the pages of the novel *Just You* and then grew into an alter ego.

She writes sweet romance set in Texas. Her books are part of the Phrey Press imprint.

facebook.com/remiromance
x.com/phreypress
instagram.com/phreypress

Printed in Great Britain
by Amazon